Turpin's Assassin:
Hero. Highwayman. Legend.

RICHARD FOREMAN

© Richard Foreman, 2021.

Richard Foreman has asserted his rights under the Copyright, Design and Patents Act, 1988, to be identified as the author of this work.

First published in 2021 by Sharpe Books.

TABLE OF CONTENTS

One	1
Two	6
Three	13
Four	19
Five	26
Six	35
Seven	45
Eight	54
Nine	59
Ten	66
Eleven	75
Twelve	88
Thirteen	95
Fourteen	101
Fifteen	111
Sixteen	115
Seventeen	17

TURPIN'S ASSASSIN

"Charm strikes the sight, but merit wins the soul."
Alexander Pope.

"Each man goes his own byway to heaven."
Daniel Defoe.

1.

At least there was no danger that the chestnut mare could be Black Bess - and its rider Dick Turpin - Oliver Sterne thought to himself, in relation to the figure pursuing the coach. *Turpin.* Everyone had heard of Dick Turpin, but few apparently were familiar with his face. Everybody asked about the outlaw whenever the coachman mentioned his profession. Had he ever seen the highwayman, or been held up by him? As if it would prove a badge of honour to have been one of his victims. Is it true that when he robbed the Earl of Sussex, the thief gifted his wife a silver brooch, as opposed to stealing her jewels? Women were reported to have swooned at the sight of him – and not because it was a hot day, or their corsets were drawn too tightly. Was he really a crack shot with pistol and carbine alike? Did he really best Peter Moulsey, the Duke of Cumberland's fencing master? Was he a gentleman, a wit and poet? Some laughably attested that Turpin had made a pact with the Devil, so he would never be caught. Others maintained that God was on his side and protected him. That he took from the rich to give to the poor. Rumour and falsehoods spread like the plague. The truth was lame in comparison, unable to keep pace. Too dull to be listened to, Sterne thought. Was Black Bess really black? - Some of the more dim-witted sots would ask. Sterne offered up a question, rather than any answers, when replying: "Did you know that Turpin was part of the Gregory gang, when they burgled Earlsbury Farm? Turpin is no Robin Hood. His code is violence and villainy, if he can indeed be judged to possess a code. Pamphlets and penny ballads are filled with the heroic deeds of Dick Turpin. But mark me. All the highwayman cares about is filling his blood-soaked purse with gold. His soul will be damned to hell, which is not to say that he should not suffer in this life, as well as in the next."

Half of England seemed deluded about the scourge of outlaws terrorizing the king's highways – and they were more deluded about Dick Turpin than anyone else.

Sterne's long-time friend and business partner, Toby Purbeck, sat next to him, spurring his team of geldings on. The two men were former soldiers, veterans of the Spanish War of Succession. They had survived the battles of Blenheim and Ramillies. Surely, they could survive an attack from a solitary highwayman. The soldiers had used their savings and booty to set themselves up with a stagecoach - to ferry the good and the great (and anyone willing to pay). Their chosen route was London to Essex and back.

"Is he gaining on us?" Purbeck breathlessly asked, focussing on the road ahead, sweat dripping down his wrinkled pate in the afternoon sun.

The coachmen knew that they would be accosted at some point. The surprise was that it had taken so long. The king's highways increasingly belonged to the knave. The soldiers agreed beforehand to flee if they could – and protect their passengers. But if they could not flee, they were determined to fight.

"No," Sterne answered, with a hint of confoundment. A footpad could have closed on them with greater alacrity. Either the highwayman's mount was fit for the butcher's yard - or he was prudently keeping his distance, due to Sterne levelling his carbine at him. Was the rogue daring and tempting him to fire whilst out of range?

The coach was rattling up and down – and side to side – to boot. Sterne struggled to hold his weapon steady. The horse's hooves – and the carriage's wheels – churned up plenty of dust. Hopefully, the highwayman might choke to death, Sterne thought. No doubt their passengers were rattling around too, like a couple of pebbles inside a boot.

"Damn you, man! Shoot the cur!" Augustus Gosset bellowed, from inside the cab.

Gosset was a sixty-year-old banker, travelling with his mistress, instead of his wife. Sterne judged that Gosset was bringing the strumpet up from London to his country house in Cambridgeshire, whilst his wife was absent, visiting her family. Sterne hoped that the banker treated his customers in a more honourable manner than he treated his spouse, but it was doubtful. Augustus Gosset was curmudgeonly, haughty and lecherous. He was quick to offer-up sermons and criticisms, rather than tips. On more than one occasion he had threatened not to pay in the past, citing poor service. Gosset was not the worst passenger the coachmen had ever encountered - unfortunately. Many in the merchant classes now rivalled the aristocracy in wealth. It was just a shame that they often failed to rival them in exhibiting good manners.

"You promised a safe and comfortable passage!" Gosset added, his face as red as the port he had been drinking, his wig comically askew.

At least the sudden drama had stopped the whore's incessant giggling - cackling - Sterne thought to himself. Although it might prove scant consolation, given the imminent prospect of being wounded or killed.

Nathaniel Gill snorted, similar to his chestnut mare, Rosie. It was clear that the coachman would not be drawn into prematurely firing his carbine. So be it, the former stable hand from Southwark mused. There was more than one way to skin a cat - or rob a coach. Gill kicked his heels into his mare's flanks to close on the coach a little, but not too much. The highwayman, no older than twenty-five, narrowed his eyes, either in concentration or to lower the odds of being blinded by the cloud of dust in front of him. Black, bushy eyebrows, like two large caterpillars, could be seen over his mask. Gill was well-built. His dark coat was stretched over his round shoulder. His stained, white shirt was stretched across his barrelled chest. A couple of flintlock pistols peeped out of the deep pockets of his long coat. A loaded carbine was sheathed in a specially made compartment of his saddle. Gill licked his lips, in anticipation that the cab would be home to some wine, ale or gin.

The sun, as polished as a gold sovereign, blazed down, chequering the ground in light and shade as its rays poured through the overhanging trees. A track ran through the woods, parallel to the main road, just behind the treeline. It would soon join the highway. There was an inn, not ten minutes ride, up ahead. If they could just maintain the stalemate, Sterne thought. Hopefully, their pursuer would be aware of the inn too – and the dog would give up the chase. Sterne glanced at his friend, who was a little older than him. Purbeck had taken the new recruit under his wing in the army. Grey hairs sprouted out of his ears – and a large mole on his forehead. His jaw was fixed determinedly. His knuckles were white as he gripped the reins of his four beloved geldings, Caesar and Brutus, Drake and Raleigh.

His bones shook, as Purbeck felt every stone and rut beneath the wheels of the mud-splattered coach. The highwayman closed. The sun retreated behind a flock of clouds. Sterne gripped the carbine tighter, scrivener-focused, wrestling to hold the weapon steady. The former infantryman was no stranger to death and the smell of powder. He had always aimed his weapon at the insidious French, however – never a fellow Englishman. He was willing to fire upon his countryman, though. It was preferable to kill, rather than be killed. Sterne's finger gently kissed the trigger. Ideally, he would like to strike the man, and avoid hitting nobler creature beneath him. The stock of the weapon nestled into his shoulder. The juddering report of the carbine would be harsh, but not unfamiliar. The coachman focussed on the approaching target, ignoring the carping and bleating noises from inside the cab.

Nostrils were flared on both man and beast. Gill and Rosie began to sweat too. The outlaw thought that he was now in range. If the coachman was a decent shot, he had a decent chance of hitting him.

Purbeck called for his team of sorrel geldings to give one last push, spitting out a gobbet of phlegm after doing so. They would be safe. Soon.

The sound of the shot shattered the air like a thunderclap. Brutus whinnied - but stuck to his task. Sterne's carbine flew out of his hands. Smoke exhaled from the pistol. Breath misted-up the air from the large, black mount which kept comfortable pace with the carriage. The rider had timed his ambush perfectly, blindsiding his target, as he rode along the track in the woods and joined the highway, just as the coach sped past. It had been an incredibly lucky or skilful shot, Sterne judged, to disarm him, as the initially disorientated coachman beheld the black-clad horseman, holstering one pistol and drawing another. His hazel eyes, above his mask and beneath his cocked hat, seemed to smile, in triumph or amusement. The highwayman on the chestnut mare was now riding alongside the coach. Gill drew his weapon and levelled it at Purbeck. His confederate aimed his pistol at Sterne and spoke. The coachman thought his tone firm and fair, reminding him of the better officers he served under in the army.

"Pull on the reins, or I'll pull on the trigger."

Turpin.

2.

As to their plan, discussed beforehand, the highwaymen led the coach, with their captives inside, to a nearby patch of ground just off the main road. Turpin invited the coachmen and their passengers to leave the cab. Anyone traversing the main road would have assumed the coach party was just taking a respite from its journey.

Gill tethered Rosie and Black Bess to a tree, not that the well-trained horses would have ever absconded from their riders. Turpin calmly aimed his pistols at the coachmen, who understandably appeared more than a little unnerved. Anger simmered beneath a mantle of worry, however, like lava coursing through their veins. The two old soldiers shared a look, but it was one of defeat, as opposed to displaying a determination to fight.

Oliver Sterne took in the famous, or infamous, highwayman. From his voice – and what he could discern from his face - the outlaw was no older than thirty. He was of medium height, slender but not rake-thin (in contrast to his confederate, whose paunch revealed how he must have eaten and imbibed most of his ill-gotten gains). His eyes were bright – intelligent; they often flickered around like a hawk's. His mud-freckled black boots were expensive. His black shirt was made from expensive linen. His hat was as black as Newgate's knocker too, devoid of any trim. Hopefully, the rogue would one day see Newgate's door, before dangling from the hangman's noose. The only splash of colour, to off-set his dark garb, came from the polished brass buttons on his coat. And a wedding ring on his finger. A sword, which might have cost Sterne a third of a year's wages, hung from Turpin's left hip. He was nigh-on dressed like a gentleman, the coachman judged. Rumour had it that Turpin had won the sword in a duel, against a Spanish aristocrat.

"I can see the point of this sword, but not the point of your existence, the highwayman joked," the turn-pike builder had reported, as Sterne overheard him at the tavern. Again, it was just rumour. But it was possible that some of the rumours about the outlaw could now be true, Sterne speculated.

The commoner was uncommonly charming, in relation to their female passenger. Turpin put the young woman at ease, as he held her hand while she stepped out of the cab.

"Thank you," Hester West said, flashing a smile and a milky calf, as she lifted her skirt a little.

"Courtesy costs nothing, but it is priceless," Turpin replied, his mask altering shape a little as he smiled beneath it.

She could easily fall out of her dress, should she fall from the coach, Sterne fancied. Her cheap perfume could even be smelled above the gunpowder and horseshit.

Hester placed a protective hand over her necklace as she stood before the renowned thief. Again, the outlaw put the banker's mistress at ease.

"Rest easy. I am not hear to unburden you of your valuables, my lady," Turpin said, realising that her jewellery had little sell-on worth. "A woman's beauty and virtue are her greatest assets. You will still be in possession of both once this ordeal is over," the highway added, reassuringly, resisting the urge to comment that she may have lost her virtue some years ago.

Augustus Gosset either grunted at the effrontery of the brigand flirting with his mistress, or at the fact that he was seemingly succeeding. Turpin, observing the insult the banker was experiencing, moved closer to Hester and whispered into her ear:

"You are an actress, I presume? I imagine you must be a good one, to suffer this dullard's company. We are all actors and actresses, to some extent, I warrant. I just haven't quite decided whether we are taking part in a comedy or tragedy. Anyone should be honoured and flattered to have you as his leading lady, however."

Hester gently bit her lip and grinned. She was even tempted to giggle, coquettishly. Her plump cheeks grew a little flush, from blushing – or due to the wine she had consumed.

The highwayman returned to his mark and surveyed Sterne. Turpin gave the coachman credit for being brave enough not to avert his gaze.

He was not devoid of courage, the outlaw concluded. The coachman was probably a good enough man, attempting to earn a good enough living. But for a few twists of fate Turpin may have well been standing in his shoes, the victim rather than the perpetrator of a crime. The highwayman was the son of a butcher. His father was keen for his boy to receive an education.

"As well as learning how to skin a carcass, I want you to learn your letters lad," John Turpin had drilled into his boy.

The son needed scant encouragement, however. The young Turpin devoured every penny ballad and book that he could get his hands on. Shakespeare, Milton and Pope were his favourite poets. He had read *Gulliver's Travels* twice, turning to the first page once more after finishing the last. He schooled himself in the ancients too, reading Plato, Homer, Plutarch, Aristotle, Cicero and Virgil. A fair amount of his booty was still spent purchasing books. The commoner even dreamed of being a playwright one day, or a satirist, as he cleaved meat from the bone and tossed sawdust on the floor, to soak up the blood. He imagined the smell of books in his nostrils, when he visited the slaughterhouse. But he soon fell into the wrong – or right – crowd. Crime paid. He had been a pickpocket, housebreaker, horse thief and footpad. His list of crimes was as long as the Mersey canal. He could barely remember when the list had only been as long as the short lengths of rope he had sold after the public executions at Tyburn. Some spectators would want a memento of the event. The young, enterprising Turpin would bring sections of rope with him for the day and pass them off as being sections of the hangman's noose. *Money for old rope*, as the saying went. The boy eventually turned to more serious and profitable crimes. A chance meeting with Samuel Gregory, when Turpin as a butcher's apprentice bought a side of stolen venison, brought him into the orbit of the gang leader. The sword was mightier than the pen, he realised. Turpin felt a sense of deliverance though when he struck out on his own. He no longer wanted to be a cog in the wheel of the brutal gang. He could now do things his way. No one would get hurt, especially women. No one would die, Turpin vowed to himself and God. As early as his fourth robbery with Gill, however, the gentleman highwayman broke his vow. A drunken farrier, Duncan Thrale, on his way home from the tavern, attacked the highwayman whilst holding up a coach. Thrale, who had recently applied to be a local constable, drew a blade and rushed the masked robber. It was kill - or be killed. If he had owned more time to react then Turpin may have shot the man in the leg, although Thrale's momentum could have still carried him to his target. Disbelief, then dejection, shaped the farrier's features. The colour drained from his countenance, nearly as quickly as the blade dropped to the ground. Thrale fell to the ground too and died soon after. A week later, when his local church held a collection for his widow, Turpin arranged an anonymous contribution of forty pounds, twice the sum he had gleaned from the robbery. "I fear that my sins will always outpace any good works I try to do, Nat," the melancholy outlaw had lamented to his friend, with an empty jug of gin in front of him. "I thought that I might endeavour to play the hero. I should have known that all heroes ultimately become tragic heroes."

Turpin was still sinning, although the outlaw told himself that he was carrying out good works by stealing from the likes of Gosset. He had targeted the banker and employed a trusted confederate to find out when the financier would be next travelling from London to his country estate.

"What's your name?" the highwayman cordially asked the coachman.

"Oliver," he replied, flatly, pursing his lips once more after emitting the word.

"I dare say that you must loathe me right now. If it's any consolation, I loathe myself even more. But we are where we are. I have no desire to kill you, Oliver. But if you prove a hindrance rather than help, I will feel little regret in pulling the trigger. I would just ask you to be patient and forbear while we go about our business – and then we will be on our way."

While Sterne interacted with the famed highwayman, Toby Purbeck surveyed Turpin's confederate. He clearly had experience dealing with horses, the coachman judged. Indeed, Purbeck was irritated by the way he retrieved a couple of apples from his bag and fed them to his geldings. Et tu Brutus? He whispered into the ears of the skittish mounts, who usually did not take to strangers, and soothed them. Purbeck also watched Gill as he entered the cab and opened their passenger's bag. Gill nodded to his companion - satisfied at their haul.

Augustus Gosset could live with the prospect of someone stealing his mistress away. But not his money. His complexion grew as red as radishes. The banker adjusted his wig, puffed out his chest (albeit his stomach still protruded further) and spoke:

"You will pay for this," Gosset asserted, after harrumphing - as splenetic as a priest, suffering from gallstones.

"On the contrary, it appears as if you are paying for this," Turpin playfully retorted, after Gill showed him the contents on the bag.

Gosset shook his jowly head. The banker was not a man accustomed to being defied. He had spent most of his life issuing orders, not obeying them. Despite often proclaiming – boasting – how he was a self-made man, Gosset had been given a loan, by his uncle, three decades ago to set-up his first business venture. He purchased a bootmaking business and, through a payoff to an old school friend, secured a government contract to produce boots for the army. Utilizing the profits he made from the lucrative contract, Gosset set himself up as a banker. He proved himself a good judge at targeting businesses which were on the cusp of failing. He was a wolf, amongst sheep, the predatory financier told himself. He provided loans at exorbitant rates of interest and, when the business owners were unable to meet their repayments, he would buy the companies outright at a favourable price and then sell off the assets, piece by piece. Gosset had forgotten the number of times he had repossessed houses and business premises. His ambition now was to purchase a peerage. If only his spendthrift of a wife had the good grace to die, he could marry into a suitably desperate aristocratic family, in need of a husband for their daughter (and in need of capital to fend off the bailiffs from securing their estate).

"You should not believe your own press. You are nothing but a common thief. Vermin like you believe that the law is something to be sniffed or laughed at," Gosset said, spittle emitting from his mouth like spray from a whale's blowhole.

"No, I think that life is something to be sniffed and laughed at. Life is a joke, whose punchline is death. But I concede that it can be thoroughly exhausting, laughing at everything," Turpin replied, his smile faltering beneath his black handkerchief.

Sterne noted how, occasionally, the highwayman's voice slipped. His clipped accent, akin to a gentleman's, lost its edge and the low-born Londoner could be heard.

"You crave fame. But the name you have made for yourself will be your undoing too. I will ensure that the price on your head is doubled. You have made a dangerous enemy today," Augustus Gosset stated, bristling with fury and self-importance.

"I neither crave fame, or infamy. Both will hasten my demise. Right now, I crave a half-decent measure of porter, a pork chop with the fat still on, and a woman with the figure – and morals – of Cleopatra. I will not lose any sleep over you becoming my enemy. You will have to get in line on that front. Poverty used to be my enemy. Now it may be injustice or boredom. I fear it is more the latter. Your reputation precedes you too, you should know, like the owner of a wet dog can smell the creature before it enters the house. Your rates of interest would make a Jew - or Scotsman - blush. You have turned widows out of their homes and threatened to sue tradesmen who you owe money to – vowing to ruin them, unless they cancel the debt you owe them. It seems that you are also a perpetrator of crimes of fashion. That wig could not even have been in style when you first purchased it. You are a perfumed shit, wrapped in a silk shirt," the highwayman posited, making no attempt now to conceal his contempt for the banker. The outlaw was baring his teeth, like a growling dog about to attack, as he raised his polished pistol. Turpin's expression turned from one of amusement to menace, as quick as a muzzle flash.

For a moment, Sterne thought that the highwayman might take a step forward and coldly shoot Gosset in the head. For a moment, such was the rictus of terror on the banker's semblance, the coachmen thought that he might release the contents of his bowels. The colour drained from his face, much like the piss could soon drain from his bladder. Gosset cowered and whimpered, like a cur about to be scolded. Turpin's confederate came between them, however, as he liberated a couple of gold rings from the banker's sausage-like fingers.

Turpin's mood and features relaxed once more and his fleeting moment of bloodlust, if it had indeed been bloodlust, vanished. He went about his business of attaching the banker's bag to his saddle – and whispered another sweet nothing into the ear of the trollop, to the further annoyance of Gosset. Perhaps recalling the trauma of having a gun pointed at his head, the would-be plutocrat merely mumbled something under his breath, rather than criticising the murderous outlaw out loud.

Before mounting his black mare, Turpin addressed his victim one last time:

"You might be now tempted to refuse to pay these good men here for their time. I would warn you not to give in to such temptation. Instead of taking the rings from your fingers, I will take the fingers from your hands. You will be a banker, unable to count his money or sign-off loans. Do you understand?" Turpin threatened, his voice as hard as the iron casing of an army cannon.

The banker sheepishly nodded, in compliance.

After speaking though Turpin turned to Sterne and playfully winked, as if the whole scene were a jest or bluff. It was at that moment that the coachman realised that he would live to tell the tale of the robbery, which was what the would-be Robin Hood wanted. Hopefully, a landlord would offer Sterne a drink on the house as he recounted his tale – and fuelled the fame and rumour surrounding the gentleman-thief. Turpin was as much of a showman as a highwayman, Sterne judged, as his horse kicked-up a cloud of dust and the outlaw disappeared into the greenwood.

3.

Sweat streaked their mounts. Beast and riders caught their breath. A gentle breeze created a shushing noise through the canopy of oak trees which flanked them along the road. Clusters of wildflowers freckled the scene. Nathaniel Gill took another swig of brandy from his flask, smacking his lips in visible pleasure.

"'Twas a good piece of business today," the burly highwayman enthused, as he thought about what he might spend his share of the booty on. He was starting to believe that money could indeed buy happiness. Gill promised himself he would buy a more comfortable saddle, despite the padding of his own posterior – and purchase a ride on Sally Murphy at *The Silver Buckle*, a brothel in Southwark. "Where sinning is a religious experience," a sign read inside. Gill enjoyed talking to Sally, almost as much as he enjoyed tupping her. *Almost*. He grinned, revealing a set of crooked teeth. "Crooked teeth, for a crooked heart," the sanguine highwayman half-joked. Gill was happy to play second fiddle to his friend – for half the take. The two men had been friends for over a decade. They trusted one another, like brothers.

"Aye, it was a job well done. I am not averse to robbing from the innocent, of course, but it feels somewhat sweeter to steal from those who can afford it. We are but minnows, amateur thieves, compared to sharks like Gosset. There are some crimes which will never be punished, some criminals who are put on a pedestal rather than scaffold. But I suppose nobody ever said, whilst keeping a straight face, that the world should be a fair place. God knows how much cruelty and spite would need to be unleashed into the world, until people would be satisfied that somehow justice had been done. But it is wrong to start moralising and philosophising, without having a drink first," Turpin said, with a flicker of a smile.

"Shall we celebrate? I could tell myself that I harbour some sorrows, and attempt to drown them," Gill remarked, after coaxing the last drop of brandy into his mouth.

"We should verily toast our success, but not tonight. I need to be up at first light to travel to London. 'Tis best I have a clear head, when negotiating with Colman over a fee for our loot. The old rogue will try to take advantage of me when sober. I might walk out of the tavern owing him money, if I arrive half-cut. I will be remaining in London for a couple of days or so. Marie has invited me to a party tomorrow evening. The cream of London society will be in attendance, unfortunately."

Augustus Gosset was not the only husband to court a mistress. Gill felt a little uncomfortable every time he heard the actress and courtesan's name. He had been friends with Elizabeth, Turpin's wife, for over nearly ten years. She was a good, faithful spouse. As much loyalty as Elizabeth had, the same could not be said for her husband. Turpin went through women – whether they be serving-maids or the wives of aristocrats – like Rosie went through bales of hay, Gill thought. The sport was in the chase, for the highwayman. Once he snared his quarry – and bedded them – Turpin often lost interest. The spark went out. "All objects lose by too familiar a view," the outlaw had once remarked, quoting Dryden. "'Tis best I put any catch back in the sea, for others to net."

Turpin's affair with Marie Harley was proving somewhat different, though. He enjoyed the woman's company in and out of the bedchamber. His interest had endured, his affection deepened. The actress was a renowned beauty. Her image had appeared in the London papers on more than one occasion. Marie was the daughter of a carpenter, who had been a drinking companion of John Turpin. Their children had played together in the back of the alehouses that their fathers frequented. She was working as a serving-girl in a tavern, when the theatre proprietor, Sylas Mortimer, offered her the opportunity to become an actress. Thankfully she could already read, albeit that was of secondary importance to the dancing roles that Mortimer first cast her in. She was a sensation, bright-eyed and endowed with both talent and natural beauty. Mortimer made her change her name, from Mary Hardy to Marie Harley. He bought the carpenter's daughter a new wardrobe, full of corsets and sheer gowns, which better showcased her assets. Her patron, who preferred young actors to actresses, arranged for tutors to help with elocution and etiquette – and introduced his newest talent to London society. Marie Harley soon learned how to perform when off stage too. She gratefully and gracefully accepted compliments and gifts, for services rendered. Even the critics were kind and forgiving.

"Marie Harley may have dropped a few consonants in her speech, but she raised the spirits of the audience in other ways... Praxiteles could not sculpture as fine a figure... This critic would happily sacrifice a pound of flesh to see Harley's Portia once more... Her eyes outshone the jewels she wore. Her face could launch two thousand ships."

Marie saved sufficient capital and freed herself from Mortimer's patronage, although she was understandably still willing to benefit from the patronage of others. The actress provided patronage herself, to poets and artists who were, like her, from more humble backgrounds. She penned several pamphlets on the art of acting and established a literary salon, although many of the guests were more concerned with courting the hostess than discussing literature.

Three months ago, whilst playing Ophelia, Marie spotted Turpin in the front row of the audience *("Amazingly, some might say, the accomplished and buxom actress captured the character's modesty,"* one enamoured critic commented). She invited the figure from her past into her dressing room, after the performance. If nothing else, she wanted to thank her childhood friend for how he had recently visited their old neighbourhood and treated her father kindly. Turpin had come across the old carpenter by happenstance and bought him dinner – and several drinks – throughout the evening.

"You have done well for yourself, Mary. Or I should say Marie. I can scarce read a newspaper without seeing your named mentioned," Turpin said, his eyes feasting upon the beautiful woman, as he attempted to cool any ardour he felt. A couple of strands of blonde hair hung down, framing a demure, intelligent face. Her silk gown rustled as she crossed her legs. Her skin appeared as similarly soft and translucent as the garment she wore.

"I could say the same thing about you," the actress replied to the outlaw, raising an eyebrow and a smile. "I only wish that the papers would devote as many pages to me as they do to you. The people love you."

"The audience loves a good villain. Look how long Walpole has been in office. I've known wine stains which are easier to remove. Perhaps the people love me because they haven't got to know me yet, too," Turpin drily remarked, charmingly half-smiling as he leaned against her dressing room door and placed a hand on his sword.

It was the first time, in a long time, that Marie genuinely laughed, whereas the performer usually pretended to laugh.

"I will be spending some time in London as well, for my sins. I would say that I will be paying for my sins but, thankfully, Augustus Gosset will be funding them," Nathaniel Gill said, with a lop-sided grin. "I intend to come back bow-legged, reeking of gin. My favourite perfume."

"I have heard that there are now vice societies springing up around the country, like weeds. They are keen for the wretched to be saved, paternally preaching to them like naughty children. They are calling for the dissolution of alehouses. Gambling is a sin. Thou shalt not enjoy yourself is their eleventh commandment. It is only the vices of the poor that they seem interested in condemning and suppressing, however. The vices of the rich are more refined and saintlier, it would appear. A soul earning in excess of three hundred pounds a year is not in need of salvation. I suspect that, for a vice society, you would be England's most wanted man."

"I have every intention of giving the cretins something to campaign about. May my morals continue to be looser than a harlot's undergarments."

"Amen to that," Turpin replied, ruminating how the opposite to vice may not have been virtue, but tedium. A wry smile softened his sharp, chiselled features, revealing a set of wine-stained teeth. Black curls peeped out from beneath his hat. Turpin marked old friend, thinking how he wouldn't change a thing about him. Gill was honest and good-humoured, in a world which had not been particularly kind towards him. A set of scars, criss-crossing his back, from a public flogging during his youth for a crime he had not committed, attested to the iniquity of the society they lived in. Yet Gill continued to smile in the face of people who frowned or looked down upon him. His good nature was either foolish or heroic, Turpin mused. Gill had recently called the capital the "promised land". Turpin thought it sometimes resembled Vanity Fair or the Slough of Despond, however.

The outlaw would have died for his confederate, partly because Gill had saved his life and proved that he would, literally, take a bullet for him. He had saved Turpin's life, for the first time, during a tavern brawl. He had used a table leg to strike the forearm of an Irishman who was about to thrust a broken bottle into Turpin's back. The last time Gill had saved his friend's life had been a month or so ago. A coachman had pulled out a small pistol and fired at Turpin. Gill had moved with surprising swiftness to put himself in between the bullet and its target. Thankfully, it struck one of the two pewter flasks the highwayman carried. Gill could tell a vice society that his drinking had saved - rather than damned - him.

A fork appeared in the trail ahead. The two men would go their separate ways. For now. Gill would travel to his local tavern, *The Cockpit*. He licked his top lip, in anticipation at the first mouthful of a frothy ale. He would play some cards, bet on a couple of cockfights and drink until chucking out time. Gill would either walk one of the serving girls home – or a couple of his drinking companions would half-carry him back to his cottage. Stupors are stupid. But there are worse fates, Gill told himself. Sobriety, among them.

Turpin would return home too. To his wife. Elizabeth. As he rode towards his house - situated close to the tavern and butcher's shop he owned in Buckhurst Hill – the highwayman thought of his mistress, as opposed to his wife, however. He pictured the scintillating actress, unfurled upon her sofa, reading a novel or applying her make-up. Turpin then imagined pulling a bow upon one of Marie's corset-tight dresses – and hearing her sigh a little. He wanted to kiss her perfumed skin and quote lines from Shakespeare with her. They had hired a box and attended the theatre during his previous visit to London. She had sat next to him, holding his hand (or placing it elsewhere on his person) during a performance of Milton's *Comus*.

There was very little that he did with Marie that he could envision doing with Elizabeth, which is not to say that Turpin did not appreciate his wife. She kept a good house and she oversaw many of his business interests (aside from the ones which were slightly less than legal). Elizabeth was aware of her husband's profession, but seldom commented upon it. She was aware of his other indiscretions too - but remained discreet. Their marriage, like most unions, had been more of a business transaction than love match. Once a month they would go through the expenditure and profits relating to their holdings. That would be the night when Turpin would carry out his husbandly duties of making love to his wife, albeit it was more an act of courtesy or gratitude. The last time he had closed his eyes and imagined he was with Marie. Most nights he would sleep in the spare bedroom, claiming that he wished to stay up late and read – and not disturb her. Turpin had spent even more time in the capital of late, due to Marie. In order to justify his time away from home he invested in a gun making company based in Chelsea, explaining that the burgeoning firm needed his support.

The highwayman refrained from kicking his heels into his mount or issuing the requisite whistle to turn the horse's trot into a keen canter. Despite his stomach grumbling, Turpin was in no rush to reach home. He enjoyed the contoured scenery and melodic birdsong.

It was a marriage of convenience and commerce, Turpin told himself. Their union had now lasted for ten years, although sometimes he deemed it more of a prison sentence.

4.

The day slowly slid into dusk, like honey dripping from a spoon. The horizon glowed like embers, lighting the pastoral scene. The tops of trees seemed singed. Starlings and thrushes warbled and whistled, darting through the sky like musical notes strewn across the page. The image was beautiful and melancholy. Turpin fancied that it may have been beautiful because it was melancholy.

The highwayman settled Black Bess into her stable and then ventured into the two-storey house. A bust of Julius Caesar stood outside the door, which Turpin would touch for luck whenever he headed out on a job. He sighed as he crossed the threshold – more in weariness than pleasure. Before greeting his wife, the outlaw walked up the wooden, creaking stairs and stored away his latest haul. One of the reasons why he had chosen to purchase the property over others in the village was because the house contained a priest hole, where he would be able to conceal his valuables – and his own person – should the authorities ever catch-up with the wanted criminal. To further avoid capture, Turpin lived under an assumed name: John Palmer.

Elizabeth was sitting at the kitchen table, mending her husband's other black coat. She knew she was covering over a bullet hole - but did not mention the fact. The outlaw never told his wife about his criminal activities – but she knew of them. "Ask me no questions and I will tell you no lies," he had advised, many years ago. Her features were halfway between being plain and pretty. Her figure was neither voluptuous nor slender, not that it could be much discerned beneath her apron and shapeless dress. Her expression was often timid, sheepish. Unlike her husband, her aspect seldom flashed with amusement or anger. Elizabeth glanced up and briefly smiled – in relief or cordiality – when Turpin entered the room (although he failed to see the smile as he removed his hat at the same time).

The kitchen was clean and tidy. Cobwebs and crumbs were religiously swept away each morning. A moreish smell of fresh bread and chicken stew swelled in the air and nourished his nostrils. His stomach purred rather than grumbled, anticipating the hearty meal he would soon sit down to. Elizabeth could at least satisfy one of her husband's appetites.

Pots, pans and cooking utensils lined the stone wall next to the stove. The oak beams above bowed but did not break. A small wooden cross, a gift for Elizabeth from her mother, hung next to a blunderbuss. Shelves, lined with an array of books, were also dotted around the kitchen, as they were in other rooms of the house. A home without books is like a body without a soul, Turpin believed, quoting Cicero. Book buying had become an addiction, a vice. It may have been one of the only vices, along with self-righteousness, that the burgeoning vice societies would have approved of. Turpin had even started to buy books in French. He had taken up learning the language, a couple of years ago, to impress a certain class of lady.

"Evening," Turpin said, polite and perfunctory. "How was your day?"

"Fine. I settled some bills - and visited Fanny Cleland. Her mother passed recently. How was your day?"

"It was fine, too. I did a bit of business with Nathaniel. All went well."

Things were fine, apparently. But tension and awkwardness hung in the air, as well as the smell of slow-cooked chicken, potatoes and onions. The candle was forever on the cusp of burning out completely for the married couple. Even the finest blade will begin to rust - as soon as it's pulled from the forge. Routine replaces romance. The idea of a happy marriage was tantamount to an oxymoron, Turpin judged. A husband and wife may fit together like a ball and socket joint, but it was one which ached. Wore away, over time. Turpin never raised his hand or voice to Elizabeth. He never sounded angry. Instead, he often sounded bored.

It was difficult to hack his way through the mists of time and remember what had initially prompted him to marry. The grocer's daughter was a shrinking violet, rather than a rose in full bloom, as a young woman. He recalled how she would wear her hair in a severe bun. Turpin preferred it however when she wore her hair down, although he never mentioned it. He wanted someone to keep house for him. The footpad had more pressing concerns than domestic chores. Perhaps he married the girl to save them both from a gnawing sense of loneliness. Elizabeth also needed saving from her father, who would beat the girl when drunk. Pity, rather than love, prompted his proposal. For her part, the pious girl believed that she could help Turpin make something of himself, save him from a life of crapulence and crime.

But still he drank. Still, he coveted his neighbour's possessions – and wives. Elizabeth would work as a seamstress during the day, whilst Turpin would hide himself away, reading or sleeping. During the night he would be off on a job - or spend his time at the tavern. She soon noticed too that his clothes smelled of perfume, as well as porter. Turpin told himself that he was a young blade, enjoying himself and earning coin. Of an evening Elizabeth would say her prayers – and often cry herself to sleep, as her husband stayed out again. At least she had a roof over her head, food in her belly and was free from her tyrannical father, she told herself.

Elizabeth thought that when they moved into their beautiful house in Buckhurst Hill that they could start married life anew. But, although it was a new chapter, it proved an all too familiar story. Mr and Mrs John Palmer were just as unhappy as Mr and Mrs Richard Turpin.

"We have been invited to a party, in the next village, tomorrow. Martha Russell is arranging a gathering for her husband's birthday. Would you like to attend?"

"Why anyone would wish to celebrate the life of that dullard is beyond me," Turpin remarked, as he peered over the simmering pot, containing the aromatic stew. "Oswald is as garrulous as Nestor and as pompous as a priest. Russell is so full of hot air that he might float away, like a balloon, at his party. Not that I would complain at such a fate. I am afraid I will be travelling to London in the morning for a few days too, so I will not be able to show my face. But feel free to attend, should you want to. Just be mindful to remember our cover story should anyone begin to ask questions."

"Oh," Elizabeth replied, the word tinged with both surprise and sorrow. Her expression was briefly pinched, pained, as she spoke. But Turpin's back was towards his wife, as he buttered a piece of warm bread.

Elizabeth pricked her finger on her sewing needle, suppressing the urge to scream, and carried on mending the bullet-riddled coat. There were moments when the woman felt she might snap, like bracken beneath a heavy boot, and rail or break down in front of husband. But she never did. There were moments when Turpin witnessed the dejected expression on his wife's face – and he felt like he should say sorry, for a litany of sins. But he never did.

Night descended like a wine press.

Droplets of rain pockmarked the window. The wind whistled, irritatingly, through the slightly warped frame. The top-floor rooms, located in a house on Bruton Street, were usually used by a priapic French ambassador to carry out various liaisons with mistresses and prostitutes. "The only woman in London he hasn't taken there is his wife," a secretary at the embassy had joked. The apartment was expensively furnished. Candlelight reflected off brass fittings.

A large mirror, which the current occupant had ordered should be polished every day, hung on the wall over a walnut bureau. An ornate, gold-handled toothbrush sat on the desk, which the gentleman used to complete the regimental routine of cleaning his teeth. As per the advice of France's most revered dentist, Fauchard, the fastidious aristocrat brushed his teeth with urine.

The figure in the mirror, casting an eye over his appearance and adjusting his shirt collar, was Pierre Vergier, a nobleman and former officer in the French army. A powdered and perfumed wig (from the same Parisian wigmakers used by the royal household) sat upon a large brow, a blade of a nose, serpentine eyes, pronounced cheek bones and a pointed chin. His clothes were elegant and immaculate. "Second best is never good enough," he often exclaimed.

A corner of Vergier's mouth briefly flicked upwards, in the shape of a tick, as he thought of the sport ahead. He had invited to dinner one of the only other women in London who had not seen the ambassador's love nest. The ambassador's eighteen-year-old daughter, Sophie. He had only met the girl a few days ago, after arriving in the capital. He had duly caught her eye. The officer had recounted a couple of war stories, quoted Racine and offered up an amorous look when kissing her hand. Vergier had also pretended to be engaged by what Sophie had to say, when she spoke about her favourite poets, the latest fashions and how she felt like a prisoner in a gilded cage sometimes. She was a foolish girl, Vergier thought. But, also, a pretty girl. An innocent girl. A clean girl. The Frenchman refused to bed a pox-ridden English whore, during his week-long stay in London. No, Sophie would suffice. He would enjoy deflowering her, instructing her. After their initial meeting he had written to her, blending compliments, seeming heartfelt confessions and feigned interest in his quarry.

"I know you enough to wish to get to know you more, Sophie… It is a rare, and therefore precious, gift to find a soul who one can converse so easily and intimately with."

Sophie wrote back immediately, expressing similar sentiments. The impressionable girl confessed that she had never encountered anyone quite like him. Sophie hoped that his soul was now at peace, after so many years of soldiering. She had already ordered the books which he recommended her to read.

"I pressed your letter to my face and breathed in your scent, my heart brimming with ardour and joy," Vergier wrote back, when he received the girl's reply.

Within the exchange of one more set of missives, Sophie agreed to visit Vergier at his rooms (and adhered to his advice of keeping their meeting secret from her father, for fear he might double-bolt the door of her gilded cage). The idiotic girl probably believed that she was falling in love with the enigmatic, passionate officer. *The world wants to be deceived. So let it.* Vergier was well versed in knowing what to say to a girl, to encourage her to be a woman. He knew how much wine to pour so Sophie would relax – but not fall into a stupor or slumber. But if the girl would not give herself willingly, he would take her by force. Vergier would have his sport – and take his prize. He had done so before – and he would do so again. Her father would be suitably too frightened to challenge the renowned swordsman to a duel, should he find out about their assignation. The next time he met the ambassador, he would be the soul of diplomacy – but ensure his polite smile was a little wider and more self-satisfied than when they had first met.

Pierre Vergier breathed in and wrinkled his nose in disgust, again. He felt like holding a scented handkerchief up to his nose, as he had done whilst journeying from the Thames to his accommodation. As much as he had ordered his valet, Gaspard, to place fresh flowers in the rooms, the chamber was still not free from the fetid stench of the city, which afflicted the Frenchman's sensitive nostrils. It was a mix of acrid smoke, excrement and rotting fish. The smell reminded Vergier of just how much he despised England and the English. And London, in particular. The city was full of gut-rot gin but few fine wines. Flabby-faced merchants gorged themselves on bland, stodgy food – their teeth as rotten as rust. Parts of Paris were a cesspool, Vergier conceded, but London was worse. A new circle of hell – a filthy temple, devoted to vice and Mammon. The peasants did not know their place. *The great unwashed*, as he called the mob, quoting Cicero. People were vermin. Rats. Slaves to their base appetites. The Frenchman detested how the noblemen of England debased themselves by playing alongside their gardeners and stable hands in a game called cricket. France was still the beacon of taste and refinement - civilisation - in Europe, he believed. Vergier was unsure whether he would die for his country - but he would certainly kill for it.

Thankfully, the aromas - of butter, garlic and seasoned poussin - from the kitchen started to enter the room and oust the noxious vapours. Gaspard had visited a shop, in the area of Kensington, earlier in the day, which catered for French cuisine. Verguer had instructed his valet to also insert ground-up antler horn - a potent aphrodisiac - into the main course.

As much as the Frenchman was capable of, Narcissus-like, staring at his reflection for even longer, he realised that his guest would arrive soon. He smoothed his plucked eyebrows, checked his teeth and removed a couple of pieces of fluff from his frock coat. The exacting aristocrat also looked down and scrutinised his manicured nails. Although the soldier had had blood on his hands, both literally and figuratively, in the past, they were currently spotless. Yet he would have more blood on his hands soon. There was more sport to be had. The former cavalry officer was now an assassin, despatched to London to kill. He thought of his mission - and the name - once more.

Dick Turpin.

5.

Morning.

Turpin had arranged for a driver of a hackney carriage, Jack Mead, to take him to London for a few shillings. The grizzled Mead owned a jovial air, until one got onto the subjects of toll roads, immigrants and tax rises. His leathery face would then crease, his nostrils flare and every fifth word would be a curse.

Turpin couldn't help but note how bleary-eyed the tavern owner was at first light - and thought that John Palmer might have spent the evening drinking. Although the highwayman had suffered a sleepless night, it had been due to waking from a nightmare and being unable to find some repose. The nightmare – and his febrile waking thoughts – re-lived the night of the Earlsbury Farm break-in.

It was not his first burglary with the notorious Essex gang, led by the charismatic – or brutal – Samuel Gregory. The young Turpin was intimidated by few figures, but the former blacksmith was one of them. Turpin had arranged to meet Gregory (along with other members of the gang: John Wheeler, Joseph Rose and John Fielder) at the Black Horse Inn, Westminster. Turpin also remembered having the best bacon and eggs he had ever tasted at the inn. The gang washed the food down with plenty of gin and ale. Gregory knew that drink would fuel his gang's courage and cruelty. They travelled on to Edgware and Earlsbury Farm, to rob the wealthy landowner, Joseph Lawrence. Turpin suspected that Gregory, who had worked in the area, had a personal grievance against the farmer.

The gang first captured and beat a shepherd boy, James Emmerton, at the entrance to the estate. Wheeler laughed as he thrust the muzzle of his pistol into Emmerton's callow face, causing him to whimper and wet himself. Inside, two servants – John Pate and Dorothy Street – were present, along with the owner. Gregory and his confederates entered the house, pistols drawn. The servants were bound and locked into separate rooms. Gregory instructed Wheeler and Rose to start going through the house, searching for valuables. He also ordered Turpin and Fielder to go to work on the seventy-year-old Lawrence – and interrogate him as to where any coin was hidden. Fielder pulled the farmer's breeches down and dragged him around the house. The traumatised Lawrence was then pistol whipped and pummelled with fists. Believing that the parsimonious landowner was still holding back, Gregory ordered Turpin to pour scalding water over their victim's head – and to sit his bare buttocks close to the fire. Tears streamed down the old man's cheeks, his throat sore from sobbing and begging for mercy.

The torture worked. Lawrence revealed where he kept a purse of guineas, in one of the first-floor rooms. As Turpin walked up the stairs, he heard Samuel Gregory – and a snivelling Dorothy Street – in one of the bedrooms. The gang leader was holding a pistol to the girl's head and threatening to pull the trigger, if she did not surrender to him. Turpin's skin crawled. His soul or conscience felt like it was being stretched out upon a rack. He placed his hand upon the doorknob, tempted to enter and save the girl. Words formed in his mouth – of protest, anger and intervention – but remained unvoiced. Turpin's pistol was loaded, but he had yet to take a life – and how could he even countenance killing his friend and gang leader? If Turpin dared to draw his pistol on Gregory, Gregory would not hesitate in pulling the trigger on him. Wheeler and Rose were upstairs too. Turpin would not have a chance to re-load and take on his other companions as well. The girl's screams shredded his eardrums, like shards of glass. Turpin stepped back from the door. He retrieved the purse and retreated down the stairs.

Eventually, Dorothy Street came down the stairs too, her legs nearly giving way twice. Her eyes were puffy, her left cheek was bruised, blood and tears caked her chin - and her hands attempted to hold her torn dress over her bosom. The sight of the maidservant, along with her reverberating screams, haunted Turpin. The gang's haul from the robbery totalled less than thirty pounds. The outlaw had also thought about Thomas Morris last night, further preventing him from sleeping.

"How's trade?" Turpin asked, feigning interest and welcoming the distraction, as Mead checked the bits and bridles on his horse, Samson, before they headed off.

"Not what it was," Mead replied, gently shaking his head and sucking air through his teeth. "The cost of keeping the nag goes up, whilst my take stays the same. Customers find it difficult to hold their drink and any conversation after nightfall. There are more ruts in the roads than whores on the Strand, or vicars in the molly houses. It might be easier if I lived closer into town, but then the wife would think even more ill of me. Still, I mustn't grumble. How are things at the tavern?"

"People drink more that what's good for them, which is a good thing, whether they need to celebrate or commiserate. The next time you're in, tell my manager, George, to put your drinks on me."

"You're a good man, John Palmer," Mead said, all but licking his lip in anticipation of free ale. His wife would probably stamp her feet - or throw a plate at him for returning home drunk again - but it would be worth it.

The outlaw was not so sure as to how good a man John Palmer, or Richard Turpin, was, however.

The sound – and smell – of livestock being driven into the capital woke Turpin up. Pigs, cows and sheep – they would all be lambs to the slaughter. It could have been worse, he thought. He could have woken up to the sound of a pious sermon, or bagpipes. In the distance he could see sinuous plumes of smoke twirl upwards. At other points, the smoke billowed and belched out, from tanneries and the like, merging into the grey, cobbled clouds which hung over London.

Mead pulled into some stables in Whitechapel. It was a hub for hackney carriages. He would feed, water and rest Samson before riding into central London. Turpin had lived in Whitechapel during part of his childhood. Like everywhere, there were worse and better places to live. His father was always able to put food on the table – and not just because he was a butcher. When his mother wasn't asking her husband to discipline their errant son, Mary Turpin was disciplining their daughters, encouraging them to complete their chores and develop an array of practical skills which would help them attract goodly husbands one day. Turpin smiled as he recalled how, as a ten-year-old, he had confessed to pickpocketing a brooch when gifting it to his mother. His reward? A beating from his father. A month later he pickpocketed a silk handkerchief and gave it to his mother, explaining that he had bought the "second-hand" item using his pay from working at Billingsgate Market. His reward? A hug and two sweet pastries. The lesson? Honesty is not always the best policy.

As much as Turpin was mindful of where he had come from, he did not feel the urge to visit the environs of his old neighbourhood. Ironically, given the way he was dressed, he might be mistaken for a gentleman and robbed by a daring footpad. The bag he was carrying, containing various pieces of jewellery, might swell the eyes of a thief. Turpin had carefully placed the loot within a linen shirt, so it did not clink and arouse any suspicion. There was of course the danger too that he might be recognised in his former neighbourhood. As much he could tell himself that no one would report him to a local constable, out of fear or loyalty, Turpin had no desire to put his theory to the test. He also owed it to Gill not to take any chances with their money.

Instead, Turpin stretched his legs, wolfed down some sausages that Mead kindly shared with him and visited the stables, in the half an hour or so that he had to wait before another hackney carriage driver, Thomas Woodman, was free to take him into the heart of the capital. Like Gulliver, Turpin was fond of talking to horses. They were far nobler animals than humans. But that was not saying too much. The highwayman had even flirted with the idea of setting himself up in business as a horse trader. Gill had an eye for the horses, as well as the fillies.

"I am not sure I could commit to an honest day's labour. My reputation would be ruined," Turpin had joked to his friend, talking himself out of the venture.

The violent outlaw fed a shire horse some hay. He then picked up a brush and began to groom the mount along its neck. The old horse could perhaps barely remember its prime, Turpin thought. Grey flecked its snout. His eyes and body seemed tired. It had seen enough of life to not want to see much more. Yet he enjoyed the attention of the stranger.

"I sometimes feel as weary as you, old fella. But we've always got one last ride in us, eh? I fear I am destined to be beaten in the race to win Marie, by a younger and finer horse, though," Turpin remarked, thinking of William Hervey, a rival for Marie's attention and affection. The highwayman had met the aristocrat former cavalry officer and, annoyingly, liked him. He was well-read, well-dressed and treated Marie with respect. Hervey was self-deprecating and courteous to peers and peasants alike. A rare trait for his rarefied rank. The handsome cavalry officer was the son of Sir Edward Hervey - "the scourge of the French" during the Spanish War of Succession. *The Gentleman's Magazine* reported that the eldest son of the peer of the realm was the most eligible, prized bachelor in London, if not the whole of England. William Hervey could have the pick of any woman he wanted. Unfortunately, for Turpin, he wanted Marie. Turpin told himself that he made her laugh more – and made her happy. But, ultimately, love is a losing game. Hervey was a Hyperion to his satyr. The highwayman could rob a hundred coaches and still appear a pauper compared to Hervey's wealth and prospects. "I should have some pride and not be fated to play second fiddle anymore. But Marie is a gem, of such beauty and worth, that I can still consider myself a fortunate man if I share her. Perhaps I will grow bored with her before she grows tired of me. I have already proved unfaithful to my mistress, as well as my wife." Turpin smiled, wistfully or wanly, as he thought of Molly, the comely daughter of a local silversmith. He had bedded her, the night after he had declared his strength of feelings for Marie. Drink had drowned out any notions of guilt he suffered at being unfaithful. The courtesan had been more honest, explaining that she would still see other suitors: "But you know that they mean, at most, nothing to me, Dick. You know me from my past. I want you to know me in the future too. You're special to me." The actress gently caressed his cheek and looked him directly, devotedly, in the eye as she spoke. Something that Turpin's wife, Elizabeth, had never done before.

Unfortunately, a week later, Marie caught the eye of Hervey in the audience, during a performance of *Troilus & Cressida* - with the actress playing the titular role. And the young, enamoured aristocrat became "special" too.

"Mead says that you're a good man, so that's good enough for me," the hackney carriage driver remarked as they set-off into the centre of town. Thomas Woodman possessed the unerring ability to constantly crane his neck behind to talk to his passenger, whilst also knowing what was in front of him too. The stout driver had a faint Irish accent, bushy red beard and a pronounced limp, from either gout or an old war wound.

Turpin did not quite know whether to laugh or cringe at being labelled a "good man" again.

"I will be tempted to take legal action, if he says such kind words and libels me again," the passenger joked, in response.

Woodman chuckled, whilst endeavouring to extract some burnt pieces of bacon from in between his even blacker teeth.

"So, what brings you to the wonderful shithole of London then, if you don't mind me asking?"

"Business and pleasure," Turpin replied, in earnest. "It's certainly not the wretched inhabitants," he added, only half joking.

Woodman let out a throaty cackle – and his horse seemed to whinny in agreement too.

"In terms of the pleasure, if you need me to recommend any clean brothels or eateries then just let me know. You wouldn't want to visit any places where the women are as tough as the beefsteaks they serve. I know a couple of places where the women – and cutlery – are as clean as one another. Or clean-ish."

"Have you tried any of these establishments out yourself then, Tom?"

"God no! I'm far too frightened of my wife to ever stray. It's one of the reasons why she tells me that I'm so happily married," the former farmhand from Lincoln said, mischievously, before vociferously lambasting a slow-witted carter over his right of way.

Turpin nodded and grinned. He did so as a matter of routine as Woodman continued to yammer on, whilst he took in the sights and, unfortunately, the smells of the capital.

London.

A great and monstrous thing, the outlaw thought, quoting Defoe.

Full of over half a million souls. A few thousand of those souls may even have been half decent, Turpin mused. Full of silk and squalor. The largest port in the country, serving a gluttonous appetite which could never be wholly satisfied. A stream of barges, like an unending funeral cortege, drew in Cheese from Cheshire, vegetables from Kent, wines from France, poultry from Suffolk, corn from Oxfordshire, and coal – a hell's worth of coal - from Newcastle. Coal, as black as a man's soul. The mud-coloured Thames, flowing as freely as gin, contained more corpses than fish. The pungent stench of Billingsgate drifted through part of the city, like a morning mist, and assaulted the nostrils, spewing out odours like a perennially erupting volcano. Occasionally, the smell of coffee, freshly baked bread or excrement cut through. There wasn't enough snuff in Christendom to defeat the rancidity which branded the air, like gold thread running through fine lacework. It was a wonder that the elms and willows populating the streets did not just wilt and die. Thankfully, the Fleet River had recently turned into the Fleet Market, having been filled in. Turpin could remember a time when carcasses were the least unpleasant things being dumped into the putrefying waterway, or open sewer. London. Overflowing with affluence and effluence. An ant-heap, but without the order and purpose. City of vice. A man could buy anything he wanted to in the sprawling den of iniquity – opium, exotic spices, women, boys, pineapples - so long as the price was right. The dome of St Paul's overlooked all, majestic and stoic, peering down its upturned nose at the rabble, scrabbling around like mice, below.

London was a melting pot, which could occasionally boil over. A tenth of the country's population dwelled in the capital. It sucked folk in, like moths drawn to a flame, and could frequently spit them back out again. More lambs to the slaughter. People moved and milled about its bustling areas - from Hampstead to Greenwich, Kensington to Shoreditch – going about their business, trying to earn enough money so they were a mite richer rather than poorer come the end of the month.

Weavers, writers, hacks, beggars, perfumers, pimps, actresses, tailors, tanners, clerks, clergymen, coal heavers, barbers, butlers, distillers, drapers, dockers, doctors, quacks, merchants, servants, surveyors, brewers, butchers, bakers, candlestick makers, innkeepers, ironmongers, scriveners, mercers, apothecaries, architects, jewellers, vintners, magistrates, seamstresses, turners, teachers, carpenters, cobblers, booksellers, bookkeepers, engravers, gardeners, gilders, fishmongers, fishwives, coopers, carters, constables, charwomen, silversmiths, stonemasons, musicians, conmen, politicians.

All human life was present, alas, Turpin mused.

An industrious shoeblack, his face grimier than the boots he polished, happily munched on a piece of gingerbread as he weaved through the throng to get to his profitable patch on the corner of the street. Queues of haggard people snaked out of shops selling state lottery tickets, clutching their coins to purchase as many tickets as they could afford (or ill afford). They were buying false hope, Turpin considered. But false hope was still hope. Gin sellers were predictably doing a brisk trade too, with men and women in equal number carrying an array of jugs for the vendors to fill. "One penny to get drunk, tuppence to get dead drunk," one shop advertised. Sufficed to say most customers paid tuppence. Turpin noticed one lamentable figure, sleeping by the kerb. People walked around him, like a river bending around a rock. Or occasionally a pedestrian would roll their eyes and step over the wiffy sot, his nose as large and red as a tomato. A couple of urchins amused themselves by throwing pebbles at the prostrate drunk – and laughed when he stirred, brushing his face as if he were being tormented by flies. He grunted, before snoring once more. A few hunchbacked washerwomen, dressed in little more than rags, congregated on the corner, gossiping as if their lives depended on it. It was almost a competition, as they complained about whose husband was the most bone idle or abusive. The washerwoman, whose husband was from Liverpool, won.

Turpin's wry expression broke out into a fully-fledged smirk as he witnessed a lawyer near Temple, bedecked in a new wig and fine garments, fall into a beau trap – where dirty water squirted up from a loose paving stone and stained his silk stockings. *Finally, some justice,* the outlaw thought. Perhaps the lawyer had been rushing back to his office from an assignation with one of the many whores, plying their wares and wiles, on the Strand. He should have been rushing to buy some of the new anti-venereal disease pills that were being promoted, Turpin wryly mused.

The highwayman held onto the bag on his lap that little bit tighter. The thief did not possess a surplus of trust. London was populated by rogues and chancers. If someone filched his haul, the thief could easily disappear into the crowd and a back alley. Turpin would more likely catch a leprechaun than catch up with the villain. Most men would be a Jonathan Wild, given the opportunity, he pessimistically thought.

Turpin asked Woodman to stop at the end of the Strand, remarking that he would walk the remainder of the way. The traffic was increasing, and he could use the walk. Perhaps he also wanted the genial cabbie to still think of him as "a good man," which he may not have done if he observed his passenger entering the notorious tavern, *The Crooked Spire*, in St Giles. The outlaw gave his driver a handsome tip. Such was the extent of the generous sum that Woodman was tempted to tell his wife about it when he got home. He soon thought better of it, however, believing that his other half would want to pocket half the money.

"God bless you," he exclaimed, unable to conceal his delight or surprise.

Whether as Dick Turpin or John Palmer, the outlaw believed it was doubtful that God would do so. But if He did choose to bless him, Turpin thought, He could begin by convincing Joseph Colman to offer a fair price for his loot. But not even the Almighty had the power to turn Colman into a generous soul, Turpin suspected.

6.

The Crooked Spire sat in a narrow, dog-leg-shaped alley, in between a boarded-up bakery and run-down tobacco shop, which was a front for a brothel on the floors above. Turpin noticed a couple of handwritten advertisements plastered on the board. One was for a dressmaker (who catered for the design and production of "immodest garments") and the other a clap doctor ("Will even treat Jews and the Irish"). Fading signage also advertised that Chaucer and Shakespeare used to drink at the tavern. The proprietor, one Nicholas Crabbe, boasted that he never cleaned the windows of the tavern. His patrons did not necessarily want anyone, particularly the authorities, spying on them from outside.

The door creaked open. Turpin entered. A few of the regulars turned around. He was a stranger to most, having visited the tavern just a few times in the past year, and was eyed with not a little suspicion. As well as being confronted by a fug of tobacco smoke, Turpin picked up on an air of menace, distrust and criminality. The highwayman felt strangely at home, however. The wooden floor was sticky with spilled wine, ale and even blood - from the various altercations which took place during the evenings. The musty tavern was ill-lit. Half a dozen dusty oil lamps hung, precariously, from the ceiling. Cobweb-strewn candles dotted the walls, flickering in the gloom like ailing fireflies.

In the gloomiest corner of the room, due to the landlord being instructed to remove the overhanging lamp usually present, was Joseph Colman. A candle sat on the table, which Colman would move closer to him when needed, but his eyes had grown accustomed to the dark. The moneylender and fence was ensconced in an alcove, with his back to the wall, sitting across from a thief who, like Turpin, had arranged a meeting to sell certain items of loot. Standing beside the table and goblin-like figure of Colman was his enforcer, Albert Merton. Turpin thought the former boxer resembled a giant slab of flesh and muscle. He stood, sentry-like, akin a praetorian guard keeping a protective watch over his Caesar. The brutal looking Merton, broken-nosed and missing half his left earlobe from an opponent having bitten it off during a boxing bout, was dressed like a gentleman. Rumour had it that his specially tailored long coats contained strategically placed copper plates in the lining, to deflect any knife attacks. A few gold rings glinted on his fingers, though one could argue he wore them for practical rather than decorative reasons. The rings could open-up a man's man face, as easily as a butcher's knife. His brawny arms were the size of most men's legs. He was rumoured to have horse-whipped a man – an informer – to death once, switching hands halfway through the punishment. Merton briefly surveyed Turpin. Unamused. Unimpressed.

Colman offered the highwayman a subtle nod, acknowledging his arrival. The gesture was neither polite nor rude. Just business-like. The gesture also communicated to Turpin that he should sit down and wait. Which he did, after ordering up a drink.

No one knew quite how old Joseph Colman was. He could have passed for fifty or seventy. He wore a middling expensive wig, which partly shielded his profile. A cocked hat hung low down over his brow, partly shielding his already hooded eyes. As much as Colman liked to read people, judge them, he did not like it when others attempted to read him. Turpin thought that the hawk-faced fence resembled a character from a Hogarth painting, but one which resided in the background. No one quite knew how many stolen items had passed through his hands over the years. He had been coming to the *The Crooked Spire*, on a Monday to Wednesday, from dusk till dawn, for over five years. No one knew how the old rogue, who was rumoured to have helped Jonathan Wild run his criminal empire, occupied himself on the other days of the week. More than one regular in the tavern, who were not known for their honesty or integrity, reported that they had seen the fence enter and exit the local molly houses. None of Colman's criminal associates knew where he lived. A curious footpad, Matthew "Shanks" Millers, once tried to follow him home. With eyes in the back of his head, Colman spotted the thief - and he was rewarded with three broken fingers and a broken ankle for his endeavours, courtesy of a displeased, growling Merton. No one quite knew how many bodies had been thrown into the Thames, on Merton's orders. No one quite knew if the moneylender was Jewish or not. Turpin suspected that he often played the Jew to his audience – and even threw in the odd Yiddish phrase to amuse himself. The fence was largely abstemious, at least during working hours. He would sit and sip from his coffee cup throughout the day, until, once business was concluded, he would partake of a small glass of port. He would eat the same meals too, not deviating from his routine. On Monday he would order lamb cutlets, Tuesday beef broth and Wednesday he would eat half – no more or no less – a chicken pie. Colman dressed smartly, but not ostentatiously. Certainly not enough to draw attention to himself. He was never tempted to wear any of the stolen items he procured. He always wore a silk scarf around his neck to, as rumour had it, conceal a red mark from where the authorities or a rival criminal gang had once tried to hang him. His voice had developed a slight croak over the past year or so. Turpin had never known the combative but calm criminal to raise his voice. Instead, when things grew tense, his voice seemed to tighten, like a screw, in conjunction with his eyes narrowing.

"I prefer vengeance to anger," Colman had once remarked to the highwayman, with a flicker of a smile, like a snake darting his tongue out. "Passions should be tamed, exploited, rather than inflamed."

Turpin had first encountered the wily fence when accompanying Samuel Gregory to the tavern. Gregory always left cursing the "Shylock," feeling that he had been fleeced. "The bastard wouldn't know a fair price, even if it struck him like a bolt of lightning." But Gregory always returned.

A blade of light cut through the far end of the room, from a half-closed door which led out into a small courtyard. Every now and then a raucous laugh, cheer or curse would sweep in, like a gust of wind. Half a dozen patrons were outside, playing a game. A cock had been tied to a stake. The participants took turns in throwing a cudgel at the bird. Whoever killed the petrified creature would win it as a prize.

Turpin rolled his eyes in response to the spurts of noise emanating from the courtyard. He then peered around the inside of the tavern, partly to assess if anyone knew or recognised him. Fame was a double-edged sword. The bounty on his head stood at two-hundred pounds, a tempting enough sum for anyone.

"If it gets any higher, I will turn myself in for the handsome reward," the highwayman had joked to Gill the previous month.

A rival fence, one Isaac Penton, sat in the opposite corner to Colman. A somewhat dishevelled, inebriated drab was slumped upon the table beside him, an arm outstretched as if she had fallen asleep whilst reaching for one last drink. Her tongue lolled out of a mouth framed by two dimples. Her caked-on make-up was beginning to crack, her hair dye beginning to run. Penton was a former quartermaster, who "fought and fucked" his way across Europe and back. He now employed soldiers to act as highwaymen. His voice sounded rough, even when he was sober, like he had been gargling with pieces of granite for half his life. His face was as cantankerous as his voice too. Penton would often stare across at his fellow fence, envying Colman for the amount of business he was conducting. Penton gazed over at Turpin too, as resentful as a spurned lover. Although the crabby old soldier did not know who Turpin was, he knew that the stranger with the bag was choosing his rival over him to fence his valuables.

Turpin's attention was diverted away from the fence towards a bald, middle-aged man who let out a brief groan, whilst rubbing his jaw.

"Bastard toothache," he exclaimed, to himself or anyone who cared. Which they didn't. He then downed a brandy, hoping to numb the pain, before proceeding to rub his pox-riddled groin.

On a few tables down from Turpin sat two burly rogues, who looked like cousins or brothers. They possessed the same lantern jaw, greying stubble and flat, porcine nose. Turpin was not surprised to glimpse a knife and cudgel tucked into the waist of their trousers, beneath their long coats. The highwayman fleetingly thought that they may be serving as additional protection for Colman, as the pair often stared at the fence as he conducted his business. They would avert their gaze, however, when Merton stared back at them. The ale-swilling pair knew where they were on the Elizabethan chain of being.

Preferring to dwell on fairer things, Turpin allowed Marie to fill the stage of his mind's eye. He flirted with the idea of buying her a gift - or presenting her with a poem. With other mistresses, the thief had just lifted lines from other poets and claimed them as his own. Marie was as well read as himself, however. It was one of the reasons why he liked her. Or loved her. She would catch him in the act of his larceny. She would either laugh or raise an admonishing eyebrow, he imagined. Turpin's thoughts grew as gloomy as the room when he reckoned that any gift he could purchase would pale in comparison to the love tokens Hervey could afford. It may be best to get her nothing, rather than prove second-best. Again.

Colman took a sip of coffee and fastidiously straightened the cutlery on his table after finishing his meeting. With another nod of his head, he summoned Turpin over. Unlike many of the other footpads, thieves and housebreakers who sat opposite him, the fence liked the highwayman. The young man, who had lifted himself up through a life of crime and life of book learning, was as familiar with poetry as he was with powder-flashes. He knew when to haggle and when to accept the right price during their negotiations. He knew when to laugh at himself and the world. It would be a shame when the authorities finally caught up with him, Colman lamented. But not even Black Bess could outpace his fame, or infamy. The reward on his head would swell, ripen – ready to be plucked. Figures such as Turpin burn bright, but burn out, the wily fence judged. It was not about mustering the courage to carry out the next job. It was about mustering the courage to retire. Turpin may have imagined his enemy to be boredom, but he would need to be boring. Live the quiet life. Samuel Gregory had been a cannon, waiting to explode in his own face. Colman hoped that Turpin would not suffer the same fate. But the odds were against it. The great eye of the hangman's noose was staring at the highwayman, patiently waiting for him to arrive. His head would fill the hole, as surely as a hand fits into a glove.

Turpin eyed the fence's business associate, or victim, who had just left the table. He looked like he had lost a pound and found a penny.

The thief appeared as if he had been robbed. The highwayman placed his bag on the round, oak table and sat opposite Colman, as he had done so over a year ago, on first transacting business with the Shylock.

"You do not altogether trust me, and I do not altogether trust you, Richard. But at least we already share some common ground. There is one thing you should know. I will always deal plainly and honestly with you and give a good price," the fence remarked, lying.

Turpin had experienced Colman's negotiating tactics first-hand during the past year or so. The fence would often purse his lips, shake his head and shrug his shoulders – the soul of being underwhelmed – when the highwayman drew out his most prized piece of jewellery. He had become familiar with several stock sayings:

"This kind of item would have been more valuable two years ago… There must be honour among thieves, else we are all damned… I will take it off your hands, partly as a favour to you and to cement our relationship… If I offered anymore, I would likely make a loss rather than profit… I may know someone interested in this, but if he does not bite then I may be left holding onto it for some time. But I will incur the potential loss and take it…"

Colman invariably came out on top at the end of any exchange. Occasionally he would seemingly capitulate to his opponent, to grant them a sense of triumph. But any victory was a Pyrrhic victory against sage fence. One of his most renowned tactics was to only offer his highest price whilst the seller sat at the table. Should he leave and return then Colman would automatically offer ten percent beneath his original fee, to encourage his associates to accept his original offer.

Turpin noticed the print staining Colman's fingertips – and a pile of periodicals (including *The Gentleman's Magazine, The Lloyd's List* and *The Spectator*) piled up beside the old rogue. The old rogue liked to remain informed. "He who increaseth knowledge, increaseth profits," the fence advised. He liked to know what was going on in the world, in case it could have an impact on the underworld. Colman also liked to know more about the person sitting opposite him than they knew about him. Turpin had once asked him if he read novels, as well as various newspapers and magazines.

"The pages of novels are best used to wipe one's arse with. Novelists present the world as it should be, not as it is. Such pretty, mendacious books are a waste of time reading – and time is money."

Turpin was just about to speak, to open the conversation, but Colman raised a hand and his coffee cup to his lips to take another sip. He removed a couple of crumbs from the table and finally, after forcing the most cursory of polite smiles, spoke:

"It is good to see you again, Richard. You have been busy, if the various stories in the newspapers are to be given any credence."

"You know better than most not to believe everything you read in a newspaper. I am grateful for their flights of fancy, though, when it comes to printing inaccurate accounts of my physical appearance. I warrant that I would not recognise myself in the mirror, if I trusted their eyewitness accounts as to what I look like."

"Indeed. I read one story which cited that you were one of the finest blades in England."

Turpin smiled, nearly laughed. Nearly spat out a mouthful of porter.

"At best, I may be one of the more competent blades in Essex – but that is largely down to a lack of competition," the outlaw remarked. His self-deprecating modesty masked a sense of pride and accomplishment, however. Ever since he was a youth, practising his strokes with a poker, Turpin had been keen to improve his skills. The sword was the weapon of a gentleman, the butcher's son believed. He imagined he was Hector – and Hamlet. When he could afford to do so, Turpin had paid a fencing tutor to test him further and hone his abilities.

"If the newspapers are to be believed, London is currently playing host to the finest blade in France, one Pierre Vergier. He is alleged to be the finest gentleman in Paris, albeit that may be due to a lack of competition too."

Turpin nodded - but was tempted to shrug or yawn. He knew that he could only ever play the gentleman. Civilised society would never allow Dick Turpin, or John Palmer, into its ranks. Even if he robbed an aristo of all his wealth, he still would not be able to buy his way into the certain clubs.

"I worry that you may soon make the society pages, as well as those devoted to crime. Oh, what a tangled web you will weave, should you draw attention to yourself as the consort of Marie Harley," the fence warned, raising an eyebrow. The married man, who frequented molly houses, knew only too well how difficult it was to live a double life. Turpin tried not to react to the news that Colman was aware of his relationship with Marie. He had observed the outlaw and the famous actress at the theatre earlier in the year. The highwayman, dressed in clothes that the courtesan had doubtlessly picked out for him, appeared enamoured. Vulnerable. Nothing good could come from the affair, Colman assiduously judged. The woman would ultimately dispose of him, like last season's fashions. But perhaps it is good that hearts get broken every now and then, the cynical criminal sagely mused. It at least meant that a man possessed a heart. Actresses' hearts could be bought, as easily as a lottery ticket. Marie Harley's heart would just cost more than most. The wily woman would justly sell it to the highest bidder – but that would be Sir Edward Hervey's heir, rather than to the butcher's son. Turpin would happily continue to deceive himself that he could win her. False hope is still hope. The young man was being played for a fool, Colman imagined. But to be wise and love exceeds man's might. "I would just like you to stay one step ahead of the law. It would be a poorer world without you, Richard. Far more importantly, I would be poorer without you. With that in mind, let us take care of business, as business takes care of us," the fencer added, reminding himself that time is money.

Turpin commenced to pull a series of valuables – brooches, watches, earrings, a silver penknife, a pair of gold-rimmed spectacles, and a couple of porcelain figurines – from his bag. In response, Colman commenced to purse his lips, shake his head and shrug his shoulders.

"'Tis a pretty piece," the fence remarked, when appraising an ornate, sapphire encrusted brooch. "Alas, it's also pretty common nowadays. Two have passed through my hands this month alone. But I would be willing to still take it should you be short of funds."

Colman quoted a price. It was Turpin's turn to now purse his lips and shake his head. Unlike other thieves, the highwayman could afford not to be desperate and accept the first offer. Turpin also knew a fence in Blackfriars that he could show his haul to.

Negotiations continued. Colman was impressed with the quality of some of the items, but he hid it well, as was his custom to do. He also concealed his frustration and disappointment at Turpin declining to sell at the prices he offered. Colman started to miss Samuel Gregory. He was much easier to deal with. He had little appreciation for beauty and the finer things in life. Much to his chagrin, the fence began to raise the sums he offered the outlaw. Not that he was entirely desperate, but he also tried to soften his opponent up by being friendly - and feigning an interest in his life.

"And how is your partner in crime, Nathaniel?" Colman asked, as he topped up his companion's tankard.

"Nat will soon be drowning in ale. He will also be suffocating in some drab's bosom. Therefore, he will be as happy as a dog with a bone. We have had another good month," Turpin said, perhaps partly to stress how he did not need to acquiesce to any of the fence's low offers.

A particularly loud brace of groans emanated from the bald patron in the corner. Turpin neither knew nor cared if he was currently bewailing the fate of his tooth or groin, but he nonetheless let the man's ululations subside before speaking again.

"Is it me, or do we have an audience in the shape of those too rogues in the booth, who seem fond of staring at us? They were keen on observing your previous meeting too. Should I be worried?"

"Allow me to do the worrying for you, Richard, in relation to that pair. And I will not even charge you for the service. The pleasure will be all mine in dealing with them," Colman whispered, his voice laced with mischief and malice. His eyes narrowed and somehow seemed to curl up at the end, like a pair of Arabian slippers, in a subtle smile as he spoke. "But tell me, how is your good wife, Elizabeth?"

"She is fine, thank you," Turpin replied, after an awkward pause. He shifted in his seat a little, feeling a twinge of discomfort and dejection. His skin crawled. The outlaw never wanted his wife to be part of this world, even to the point of hearing Colman mention her name.

"My apologies. I did not mean to pry. I was not expecting you to paint a picture of marital bliss. Show me a happily married man and I will show you a walking corpse, or honest politician."

7.

The two men concluded their business. Turpin ordered a large brandy. Colman celebrated by ordering another coffee, but this time spooning an additional sugar into the beverage. As his next appointment was running late – "I cannot abide tardiness or dishonesty; he will pay, through me paying less" – the fence invited the highwayman to sit with him and share any news or gossip.

Turpin disclosed the details of his last robbery – and victim. He could seldom remember an instance of the dispassionate Colman grinning so fulsomely.

"The sense of shame and loss that Gosset is experiencing could not happen to a more ghastly man. I shall be almost evangelical about spreading the word, concerning his misfortune. Finally, a banker has an unprofitable day."

In return, Colman informed Turpin of some news concerning one of the fence's rivals, Percy Waller. Waller, a former stonemason, had been drawn into Jonathan Wild's orbit during the previous decade. The wealthy criminal now had pretensions of being a gentleman – and had recently paid to arrange for his family to have a coat of arms.

"He has placed a number of tools from his previous trade on the coat of arms, one of which looks like a giant phallus – which is apt to represent him."

Colman also mentioned that he had recently attended a new production of Christopher Marlowe's *Doctor Faust*, featuring the handsome, but witless, actor, Granville Perrott.

"He is overrated. And he overacts, even more than the landlord here overcooks his cutlets. Perrott seems to be of a school of acting where one shouts one's lines, in contrast to speaking them. I dare say that the audience in the cheap seats – in the adjacent theatre even – could hear the popinjay, as much as they would have preferred not to."

Turpin smiled and replied:

"I may well hear Perrott this evening myself, as he will likely be attending a party I have been invited to."

Upon hearing about the party, the speculator spied an opportunity.

"You will doubtless be cornered by all manner fops and grand personages who have more money than sense at the gathering, but you can turn a curse into a blessing, Richard. Let the peacocks witter on about how often they retreat to their country estates, leaving their London town houses vacant... If you are not willing to commit to any burglaries, feed me any information. I will pay you a fair sum."

Turpin maintained that he may well have a different definition to Colman as to what a "fair sum" was. Shortly afterwards, the highwayman took his leave.

St Giles was a veritable warren of alleyways and courtyards. Many a soul had turned a corner in St Giles and walked into a gnarled thug with a blade or come face to face with an even scarier looking harlot. There were certain neighbourhoods in London where you kept one hand on your purse and another on a barely concealed weapon. Gloom fell like a veil over the parish, with sunlight seldom seeping through. The tops of buildings seemed to lean towards one another, as if attempting to kiss. The usually bustling parish at night time was relatively quiet during the afternoon. The whores had yet to wake up and most of the drunks, save for the one Turpin nearly tripped over, were at home, asleep. It was also too early for most of the criminals to be out on a job. Most, but not all.

Robert Cragg and his cousin, John Gough, had been dockers from Bristol. They had travelled to London a year ago to make their fortune. They were not averse to stealing a fortune too, to better their prospects. With work on the Thames quayside proving too inconsistent – and ill-paid in relation to funding their gaming habits – the two men found themselves working as enforcers for Edgar Fisher, a fence based in Rotherhithe. Fisher had instructed Cragg that morning to visit *The Crooked Spire*.

"Firstly, I want to know how business is going for the old Jew bastard. Note the quantity and quality of what's passing through his hands. Also, if he meets with anyone who has money in their pockets or goods on them worth filching, then roll them over after they leave tavern. Don't be too bloody obvious. And don't try anything with Colman and his ape. Otherwise, you'll come hobbling back over the river – if you come back at all."

Cragg and Gough had stuck to their task, apart from perhaps avoiding being too obvious, and observed the fence doing business. The time was right to leave, however, when they witnessed one of his associates receive a notable sum in notes and coins. The thief also still possessed a number of valuables, which he had refused to sell to the parsimonious moneylender, in the bag he carried.

Low hanging fruit, Cragg thought to himself, as he left the tavern and stalked his quarry.

A sudden, chilly breeze blew down the alley, cooling the film of sweat on Turpin's brow. It would be a matter of when, not if, the rogues made their move and attacked. Had they recognised him and were aiming to secure the reward for his capture? Or were they just intent of robbing him? Were they intent on injuring or killing him? If a twenty-nine-year-old Christopher Marlowe could die in Deptford from a blade between his ribs, Dick Turpin could easily die from being stabbed in St Giles, he reasoned. *Bloody thieves*, the highwayman thought to himself, with little care for irony.

Turpin regretted travelling to the capital without wearing his sword and carrying a pistol. He could have also retrieved a blade and gun from the lodgings he kept in Cockspur Street, in Charing Cross. But he was wary of running late and earning the displeasure of the fence. Turpin also now regretted not inviting Nat to join him, for added protection. His friend would not openly complain, but Turpin's heart sank on picturing the disappointment on his face should he have to tell him about losing their haul.

He quickened his steps a little, but so did his pursuers. He was tempted to just bolt and run. Perhaps he could outpace the men or disappear into a crowd. *The Rat's Castle* on Dyot St was not far. There would be people there. Although the curs may be brazen and skilled enough to stick him and take his bag without anyone noticing, Turpin fancied. A bead of sweat stung his eye as he tried to remember the geography of St Giles. The next turn could, quite literally, lead to a dead end.

Or he realised that it may be his salvation. The end of the alley he turned into broke off into two, opposite directions. If he could put enough distance between himself and his opponents, they might lose track of him or choose to split up. *Divide and conquer.* Turpin clutched his bag to his chest and ran. Better to retreat – and live to retreat another day – than fight and fall. Turpin wanted to be a mite richer at the end of the month, compared to the beginning of it. It would be difficult to earn any additional funds if he died. He suddenly thought of Elizabeth, how he did not want to leave her in penury. He may not have been a good man, but she was a good woman. Turpin also thought that if he reached a public space – and he was still being stalked – he would relinquish the contents of his bag to strangers, if it meant that they congregated and got in the way of his two pursuers.

He ran. Hope soon turned to despair, however, as one of robbers appeared at the end of the alleyway, having ran himself to box his victim in. Turpin turned around to observe the second man, behind him, drawing a pistol. The gun may not have been the most finely crafted weapon that the highwayman had ever encountered, but it would probably still do its job, if called upon. If his only hope was that of a misfire, he was damned.

Cragg and Gough grinned, wolfishly, as they closed in on their victim. Turpin endeavoured to remain calm. He still clutched the bag to his chest with one hand - yet wrapped his fingers around his dagger with the other. He strangely heard a voice from a street balladeer break out into song, a few streets away.

"He clutched his cross and he cried Amen
As the drums kept on drumming, once more and again.
God help the soldier and God help the fool,
God help the devil - God help us all."

Gough held his cudgel aloft, his gap-toothed smile widening. Cragg had warned his friend not to kill the man, but that didn't mean that they couldn't enjoy himself by beating their prey half senseless, The sickening, cracking sound of his cudgel breaking bones was music to the enforcer's ear, far more than any song from a balladeer.

"We are all businessmen here, gentlemen. In terms of you gaining the greatest reward for the least amount of labour, I would be happy to give up the contents of my purse and bag, should you allow me then pass unmolested," Turpin remarked. As much as it may have injured the highwayman's professional pride to be robbed, he was understandably disinclined to take a beating, or worse.

"Give everything up, and you can then be on your way," Cragg uttered, screwing his face up in disdain at the coward before him. Lying. As soon as he secured the haul, Cragg would give the nod to his cousin to knock him to the ground. A few kicks to the face and a few cracked ribs would then immobilise the stranger, preventing him from following his persecutors. The beating would also put the fear of living God into the well-attired thief, dissuading him from trying to track down the robbers.

Cragg and Gough moved a couple of steps closer. The former's pistol was cocked. Although he did not want to kill the stranger, he would if he needed to. With little or no remorse. Gough gripped his cudgel even more, his white knuckles cracking. His smile turned into more of a snarl, as he bared what few teeth he had left inside his head. Gough started to think about what he might spend the profits from his loot on, after he paid off some of his gambling debts. A rat, which had somehow lost its tail, scurried along a brick wall and disappeared into a hole, perhaps intuiting that a bloody scene would soon ensue. Turpin ran through some scenarios. Offering up any valuables was unlikely to purchase clemency. He needed to do enough to escape, rather than defeat, his opponents. It would be a suicide mission to try and disarm the villain with the pistol, as he would get off a shot and hit his target at such short range. The challenge would be to assault and get beyond the vicious looking cretin with the cudgel. He could hold the bag in front of him like a shield and then thrust or stab at the man with his knife. Hopefully, Turpin would injure him severely enough for his confederate to attend to him – and he would not be disposed to continuing the chase. Hopefully, once past the rogue, the cudgel-wielding mugger would prevent his companion from securing a clear shot. Hopefully, the man's aim, as well as his weapon, would be second-rate.

Hope came from a different, unexpected source, however. As much as Turpin tried to remain stoical, his expression must have sufficiently altered as it lingered on the sight of Albert Merton appearing behind Cragg. Cragg was in the process of turning around when Colman's enforcer grabbed him by the collar of his coat and slammed him against the brick wall - twice - as if he were as light as gossamer. The bridge of his nose split open, as if it were rotten fruit. The pistol fell to the floor without, thankfully, firing. Life became, at best, a blur as he slumped to the ground. Merton's brow was crumpled a little as he attacked Cragg, but barely an iota of anger or effort registered on his impassive countenance.

Gough remained in a state of shock, or fear, as he witnessed the sudden, devasting display of violence from the hulking Merton. He hesitated, caught between fight and flight. Turpin made no such mistake, though. He took a couple of steps and buried his foot into the man's groin. Turpin then grabbed his head and lifted his knee, breaking his cheekbone. Cragg and Gough groaned and writhed in the grimy alleyway, like two drunks suffering from a bout of dysentery.

And their ordeal was not quite finished. Without a word said, Merton bent down beside both men and methodically, mercilessly broke three fingers on each man's hand, snapping the digits like a child would twigs. The cousins caterwauled, even more than the balladeer.

"Listen to me," Merton said, flatly and firmly, as he loomed over Cragg, pressing his foot down upon his ankle to attract his attention. "If you walk into St Giles again, you won't be walking out. This is your first and only warning. Tell that bastard Fisher that I won't just be coming for you, either. I'll cross over the river and will be coming for him."

Cragg nodded his head, as blood and tears wended their way down his chin.

Sunlight broke through the slate-like clouds - pouring along the widening streets, like rain washing away the crud. A couple of carters argued about their right of way, offering up insults that made several ladies out shopping blush - but other onlookers duly smirked.

"Thank you," Turpin remarked, as Merton escorted the associate of his employer out of St Giles and into Charing Cross.

"Don't thank me, thank Mister Colman. I was ready to sit down and have a late lunch, when I was asked to keep an eye on you – and those toothless mutts. My pork chop is now going to be overcooked. Seeing you alive – and no amount of thanks – can make up for that," Merton stated, though Turpin observed the flicker of an amused smile on the gruff enforcer's face. He thought that the bodyguard could well be as unreadable and sphinx-like as his employer.

"I should buy you a drink."

"You should buy me two, at least – along with a pork chop. My wife will be pleased that you are unharmed, however. The daft mare thinks you are Robin Hood re-born, the people's champion. Once a week she makes me read articles to her about your exploits. I've got a permanent bruise on my left side from where she prods me to keep reading, when I start to drift off to sleep. She will be even more pleased when I tell her that you managed to wheedle more money out of Mister Colman. I'm surprised he didn't choose to pay a couple of footpads himself to get his money back. My better half will never forgive me if I did not ask. Did you really give the wife of the Duke of Sussex a piece of jewellery, instead of rob her?"

Turpin did not know whether to be amused more by the fact that the brutal enforcer was married and seemingly under the thumb of his wife, or that the usually laconic Merton was becoming as garrulous as Nestor.

"I do not even buy my own wife jewellery. I am not about to gift any to a stranger. Grub Street hacks are prone to flights of fancy even when sober. They will never let the facts get in the way of a good story," the outlaw argued, avoiding a particularly large mound of fly-infested dung as he crossed the street.

"The newspapers seem to be relishing tales of your rise, nearly as much as they will relish stories of your demise. Mark, that you will not be the only one upset if you get caught. There are criminals who think that if you can somehow stay one step ahead of the authorities, they will too. My wife – and Mister Colman even – are cheering for you. I might even cheer for you, if you didn't keep me from my lunch so much," Merton issued, drily, with a flicker of a smile again. "Let us hope that you keep the balladeers in business for some time yet. There seems to be as many songs as newspaper articles devoted to you, of late."

"Aye, but only because there are a surfeit of puns and rhymes to be formed out of my first name," Turpin replied, permitting himself an amused smile too.

You have to laugh at life. Before you die.

Pierre Vergier yawned and then straightened his lace cuffs, as he sat at his desk after finishing off another entry in his diary. His diaries could never be published, until after his death, such was the compromising content. His words and deeds would live on, however, thanks to his diary. They would help him become as immortal as a god, the Frenchman half-joked to himself sometimes. A silver bowl of rose petals lay on the recently polished bureau. Vergier breathed in the bouquet of the tolerable burgundy which Gaspard had arranged. His valet had also arranged the purchase of the long back coat which hung on the back of the door – and for a professional swordsmith to sharpen his blade.

Still Vergier wrinkled his sensitive nose in displeasure, in response to the *English* stench which managed to penetrate the apartment. He had instructed that the windows remain closed. But still the odour lingered in the cushions, curtains, mattress and every sinew of the air – like the smell of smoke, after a fire. Even the heavily perfumed letters, which Sophie had sent that morning, could not wholly expel the foul aroma. The words were as florid as the fragrance that they were soaked in, Vergier fancied. The sentiments were trite, almost a parody. The now besotted child had sent the two long letters before midday, declaring her love. Did the naive girl not possess any pride or self-control? Vergier recalled the words of Alexander Pope, who he rated as one of the few English poets in possession any technical or satirical merit.

Nothing so true as what you once let fall,
"Most women have no characters at all."

Unfortunately, the Frenchman also recalled the words of his conquest, who must have suffered writer's cramp during the morning, as lines poured out of her like scented sewage. Page upon drear page. Perhaps he should have squeezed her hands even tighter last night, as he laced his fingers in hers, so she would have been unable to hold a pen the following morning – and spare him her heartfelt, nauseating confessions.

"Last night was the dawn of the first day of the remainder of my life... My skin still tingles, my heart is still racing... Only now do I know just how powerful true feelings are. Carnal feelings. Divine feelings... You see into my soul, my darling, like an astronomer can spy into a telescope and survey a celestial sky..."

Vergier was as equally contemptuous as he was amused. He started to realise, however, that he was becoming as bored with deflowering daughters as he was with cuckolding his rivals. Thankfully, the former officer would soon return to the activity which he never grew tired of. Killing.

As well as receiving correspondence from the Vicomte de Montbard that morning, Gaspard also handed him an invitation he had been expecting. To a party, hosted by the actress, Marie Harley. The Frenchman glanced at the headline to an article in one of the newspapers that Gaspard had purchased and placed on his desk. Pierre Vergier smiled. Gently. Seductively.

"Dick Turpin will become a living legend – or die trying."

8.

Sunshine cascaded through the window, like patrons streaming through the door, trying to secure a drink during the intermission of an opera. Marie Harley sat in her large bedchamber, in front of a polished, mahogany dressing table. Its surface was inlaid with ivory, its sculptured feet made of gold. The piece of furniture had been a present from a former admirer, or it could have been considered payment for services rendered. The actress always put on a consummate performance for her audience of one. Yawns were suppressed or concealed. She refrained from cringing, when his dry, liver-spotted hands pawed her. When she sighed, her lover believed that the courtesan was swooning, rather than emitting a sigh of boredom. An array of creams, in decoratively labelled jars, and bottles of perfume were spread out across the dresser. They were strategically placed and faced in the same directions, as if they were troops about to go into battle. All manner of accoutrements, dedicated to the trade of beauty, lay on the table too, like surgical instruments. Hair curlers. Hair straighteners. Hair scissors. Eyebrow pluckers. Eyelash curlers. Earwax scrapers. Three different types of tweezers. Nail files. Nail scissors.

Marie smiled as she thought herself akin to Belinda, the heroine of *The Rape of Lock*. The actress always dreamed of playing the protagonist in a theatrical production of the poem. She had kept the idea secret, but Turpin had once suggested it too.

Voices bubbled up from downstairs. The gardeners were leaving as the pastry chefs were arriving. Marie had confidence that her housekeeper, Gertrude, could deal with the procession of visitors, partly because she had left detailed instructions to smooth out any wrinkles in preparation for the party. She duly hoped that Gertrude had ordered the gardeners to remove their muddy boots before entering the house, otherwise her usually porcelain smooth brow would develop a few cracks, when admonishing her usually competent housekeeper.

Her blonde hair, "like spun gold" as one enamoured theatre critic put it, hung down, below her shoulders. Her locks - damp and glossy from a recent bath, when one of her maids had washed her hair – had grown fairer during the summer months. The actress was barefoot. She occasionally scrunched her toes against the thick Persian rug beneath her feet, purchased in Delhi by a former suitor in the East Indian Company. Marie wore a pearl-coloured silk gown, embroidered with gold thread, belted at the waist, with the most plunging of plunging necklines. She could still remember the sensuous experience of when she first wore silk. It was a new sensation. A new world. Semi-divine. Or divine. Mortimer had hired her out as an artist's model. The artist had made her wear the garment off her shoulders - and gifted her the dress as a thank you for services rendered. Marie recalled how she did not want to wear any other material afterwards, that it would somehow be a step backwards. She let Mortimer know that she would be willing to accept other items of silk from her admirers and would-be patrons.

Marie thought about her current patron and admirer, as she began to run a brush through her silken hair. Losing William would somehow be a step backwards. She may never find anyone as courteous, handsome, generous and (financially) endowed again. The sweet man had declared his love, on more than one occasion, and been sincere. He had even spoken to his family about his intention to marry the "lady" - whose past and reputation were dubious, to say the least, in the eyes of his mother and father. When Sir Edward Hervey said the word "lady," there was more than a hint of scorn and sarcasm in his voice. William's lawyer had recently drawn up an agreement, to pay Marie three hundred pounds a year, as a gift. William had not overtly mentioned it, but the payment was for exclusivity of access to the actress.

"I can no longer endure sharing you with anyone else," William remarked, his voice charged with passion, like a cannon full of tamped down gunpowder. "Every day apart from you is a wasted day."

William had also asked Marie if she loved him and could give him her heart. He had been on his knees as he spoke, like a character from a new-fangled novel. The ex-officer did not usually appear so melodramatic – or pathetic.

Marie told him that she loved him too, widening her eyes and squeezing his hands, similar to when she had played the part of Hero in *Much Ado About Nothing* (although she would have preferred to play the more interesting part of Beatrice). Marie could not be sure if she had truly loved anyone in her life, aside from perhaps her younger sister, Sarah, who had tragically died at the tender and innocent age of twelve. What was it to give one's heart away? It was an act of foolishness, at best, she judged. She did not love William. But she liked him. Would that not be enough? She liked him enough to please him, submit to him, even when she did not feel like doing so. To kiss him when his mouth reeked of tobacco. To laugh at his witticisms. To smile when he smiled. To be an actress, even when off stage.

The curtain billowed a little. A gust of wind ushered in some ill-smelling vapours, from a less salubrious part of the capital. Perhaps from one of her old neighbourhoods. Marie liberally distributed one of her favourite perfumes around the chamber to combat the unwelcome odour. The fragrance had been a specially concocted gift from a perfumer based in the Royal Exchange, who was an ardent fan of the "sublime and fabulous" actress.

Signing to accept the settlement of three hundred pounds per annum would not be akin to some Faustian pact, Marie told herself. She would not be sacrificing her soul. But she would, doubtless, need to sacrifice Turpin. But he must have known that they could not expect to have any substantial future together? He was already part of her past. He was already married. If Marie was honest with herself, which she was, the highwayman was a dead man walking. Sooner or later the outlaw would be apprehended, condemned and executed. Her future was with William. Marie had no desire to return to a life where she slept upon a flock mattress, with fleas and lice for company (although she had slept next to equally unpleasant creatures since, that made her skin crawl). Love was not a prerequisite of marriage. It was laughable to think so. The role of wife, or mistress even, to an aristocrat was one that any actress would dream of. William could help Marie pay off her debts (and those accrued by her father, who she did not want ensconced in debtor's prison again). A new life – and world – would be opened-up to her. She could visit the capitals of Europe and be feted in their literary salons and gilded societies. Haughty women who had once eyed the courtesan with disdain, would be green-eyed with envy. William could keep the celebrated actress in the style she had grown accustomed to. He could keep her in silk dresses.

Turpin entered his lodgings on Cockspur Street. Damp and mould were the only things still holding the building together, he surmised. The warped floorboards creaked more than an old coalminer's bones. The highwayman turned up his nose and nearly retched at the foul but familiar smell he encountered. Turpin opened the window, which the landlord was tempted to brick-up due to the pernicious window tax - and breathed in a lungful of only slightly less foul air. Turpin stayed in London a few times a month, depending on business and when he could see Marie (which was not as frequently as before, due to her being "busy" and seeing Hervey).

The one, cramped room housed a small bed (which Turpin had paid for, to replace the bug-ridden one the landlord provided), as well as a table and chair. The outlaw kept a sword, pair of pistols, some tools of his trade and a few books behind a panel on the wall. In terms of clothes and other possessions he paid the landlord's wife to clean and keep them safe (for fear she would just enter his room and pilfer them) while he was absent. Turpin kept a set of his finer clothes in London. He did not pack or wear any as a way of pretending to his wife that he was not stepping out in society in the capital or seeing a mistress. His trips to London were purely for business reasons, he would argue. Elizabeth pretended to believe him, lying to her husband and herself.

He placed his money and what was left of his haul behind the panel. A loaded pistol lay on the bedside table, along with a well-thumbed copy of Meditations by Marcus Aurelius, as Turpin looked to sleep. He wanted to be fresh for the party. Fresh for Marie. Actors and actresses, aristocrats, poets and politicians, men of wealth and standing would be attending. It was likely that Turpin would be the only highwayman at the gathering, but he would not be the only liar and thief, he fancied. Marie mentioned that she had invited Alexander Pope, perhaps as bait to net Turpin as a guest – although it might prove difficult to spy the diminutive poet in the crowd. The acclaimed novelist, Henry Fielding, could be in attendance too, albeit his latest mistress only usually permitted him to leave their bed if he took her shopping.

When Marie first mentioned the party, Turpin's immediate thought was to enquire if his rival, Hervey, would be present.

"Of course. William will be paying for the party, so it is only proper that I invite him as well… You know how I cannot abide jealousy. It is dull and destructive. If I met your wife, this cat would sheath her claws. I would have no desire to embarrass her, or myself. I need you to pay me the same courtesy."

Marie then made it clear that Turpin was being invited to the party in the capacity of a friend of the hostess, rather than her consort. He felt like he was as estimable as a slug – and her words were salt.

The highwayman closed his eyes, although the image of Marie seemed painted upon his eyelids. He soon drifted off to sleep, too tired or weary to dream.

9.

Turpin was dressed smartly, in dark calfskin breeches, silk stockings, polished black shoes (replete with buckles), a pressed white linen shirt, and a brass-buttoned, navy-blue tailored coat. If the apparel oft proclaims the man, the highwayman was a gentleman. A satin handkerchief poked out of his velvet-lined breast pocket. Wary of thieves - not just due to his experience earlier that afternoon – he kept his watch secure in the inside pocket of his coat. He refrained from wearing a wig, make-up, scent and a surfeit of jewellery. The butcher's son already felt trussed-up, like a goose in his father's shop window. He straightened his stiff collar, however, and told himself – in the ghostly reflection in the windowpane – that he was John Palmer, a successful business owner and "friend" of the hostess of the party. His false identity was as true as any other. He was well-read, as well as well-dressed. His sword was as equal in craftmanship to the next man, his fencing skills superior. He had no ambition or intention of being the centre of attention at the party, but he would not appear out of place either.

Despite the danger of stepping into a beau-trap, despite the thought of some boisterous (drunken) youths slinging mud (or something fouler) at their apparent "better", Turpin decided to walk to the party venue, located in the fashionable neighbourhood of Brook Street. The bumpy ride from a carriage may well shake the buttons off his shirt. The traffic would prove atrocious too.

Turpin chose a route which encompassed Regent and Oxford Street. The throughfares, teeming with shops and wealthy shoppers, reminded the outlaw of when he was a boy. The busy streets still proved rich pickings, for pickpockets. On his days off from working with his father, Turpin would lie in wait for a lady to faint or for an argument to erupt between carters, or for any other distraction to occur. He would then relieve a victim of a handkerchief, watch or wallet – and disappear into the crowd, like salt dissolving in water. His mother had tried to teach him, like tenets of a catechism, that thou shalt not steal.

"It's wrong. It's a sin. Nothing good can come of it," she stipulated on more than one occasion, suspecting that her child was heading down the wrong path.

A young Turpin would tell himself that his victims could afford to lose some of their wealth, that they had made their money off the backs of the poor. Now that the outlaw was as affluent as his former marks, he was not so unforgiving. Turpin's experiences as pickpocket had taught him to be aware. He had twisted the wrist and kicked the arse of more than one thief who had tried to target him. He was tempted to lecture the cherub-faced rogues and posit that crime didn't pay. But it did. The highwayman was now residing in a well-furnished house, rather than wallowing in prison or swinging from the end of a rope. He had provided gainful employment for his best friend and funded a local school with the profits from his unlawful enterprises. Good was coming from his life of sin. He was taking from the rich and giving to the poor.

Thankfully, the weather was still fine. Rain was unlikely to spoil the party, which would be largely hosted in the garden. Although Turpin suspected that his jealousy – or being cornered by a dull and vain actor – could ruin his evening.

Whereas during his journey in the morning, from east towards the centre of London, Turpin had largely encountered the lower ranks and middling sort of society, he now mainly observed the middling sort and upper ranks of London's populace. The beggars had no doubt been moved along by constables at the foot of Regent St - or ushered off by several withering looks. A few workers were trudging in the opposite direction to Turpin. They seemed as leaden-footed, careworn and hunched over as milkmaids carrying their yokes.

Shopping had become the new religion for some (particularly ladies of leisure) – and Regent and Oxford St were places of worship. A copy of a pamphlet, *Kind Cautions against Swearing*, meant for hackney carriage drivers, flapped in the curb, but otherwise the locale was uncommonly litter free. The smell of various food carts began to fill the air, displacing the ubiquitous stench of the capital. Hawkers advertised their foodstuffs:

"Chestnuts, spicier than an Indian... Strawberries, sweeter than your truelove... Muffins, as fresh as the day is long..."

One buxom woman approached Turpin and exclaimed,

"Crabs, come buy my crabs."

He merely raised a suggestive eyebrow, refraining from making any further comment. Turpin could not help but eye a number of wives – and widows – as he walked through the human tapestry of beauty and fashion. Some women coyly avoided his glance, whilst others held it, coquettishly smiling or blushing above a fan or beneath a parasol. For many, however, the allure of shop windows easily eclipsed the sight of other people.

There were half a dozen more dress shops strewn along the parade than there were just a year ago, Turpin thought – which is not to say that there was not a glittering array of other stores:

Milliners, map sellers, china shops, confectioners, cheesemongers, lamp shops, lacemakers, stationers, silk shops, watch sellers, perfumers, book shops, furniture shops, fruiterers, florists, upholsterers, jewellers, jam makers.

Shoppers cooed at the various goods on show – and not just at the items on sale – as they endlessly streamed in and out of each store, somehow managing (perhaps from practise) to not trip over one another. One wasp-waisted lady exclaimed that she would "die" if the milliners she was bustling towards had sold out of a gem-encrusted hatpin she desired. Another woman sighed, or boasted, to her stouter companion that she would have to arrange to have a dress taken in, which she had recently purchased. Turpin was not immune to being drawn into gazing – or gawping – at several window displays too. One celebrated outfitter for the "more distinguished gentleman" was displaying a smart, silver-handled walking cane, which also served as a sheath for a sword. The highwayman smiled broadly - and nearly burst out laughing - as a haberdashery advertised handkerchiefs, "Embroidered with the face of Dick Turpin". Turpin did not know how to feel about people wiping their nose with his image. At least he was not suffering the embarrassment of the item being on sale – although sooner or later he would be relegated from a prized position in the shop window to being thrown into a bargain bin.

Shopkeepers greeted customers with open arms and toothy or oleaginous smiles. Some even bowed to their regular female customers, treating them like royalty. They would be swift to offer credit to some (whilst credit would be the last thing they would offer to others). Payment was counted quickly but carefully, as counterfeit coin was rife in the capital. Turpin knew it was not just a rumour that Colman employed a dozen craftsman to produce a steady stream of counterfeit coinage.

Gaudily attired footmen, dressed in uniform as if part of some private army, burdened like pack mules with an array of bags and boxes, followed their masters and mistresses around. Many named the attendants "fart catchers," such was their custom of walking closely behind their employers. They were walking ornaments, displays of wealth. Some people imagined that the measure of a man was linked to how many servants he possessed. It may have been as good a measure as any, Turpin idly or indifferently mused. If money wasn't everything, it was nearly everything at the very least.

He had come a long way – and not just because he had journeyed from Buckhurst Hill, Turpin thought. Whilst growing up, the likes of Rotten Row, Dirty Lan and Pissing Alley had been familiar streets and haunts. He was now at home in Regent and Oxford Street. Perhaps it was due to his success as a criminal, or his determination to educate himself or become a gentleman. Perhaps it was due to the character of London and England. But a man could make something of himself in the capital - or die trying.

As Turpin turned into Oxford Street, taking a circuitous route to Brook Street, he remembered how he had once invited his wife to join him in London. He offered to buy her a new outfit or two. Elizabeth replied that she was happy to mend and make do with the dresses she already possessed. There was no pleasing her, he somewhat uncharitably thought at the time. Perhaps there was a way of pleasing her, though. By retiring from his dangerous occupation. By spending more time at home – and being a faithful husband. He dismissed such scenarios, however, brushing them away like flies in front of his face. His wife would have been pleased if they could have children. Elizabeth blamed herself for their marriage being childless. She had even suggested, one teary night, that her husband should leave her. Turpin was ashamed that his wife would think that ill of him, that he would abandon her because she could not give him a child. He comforted and reassured her, as best he could. Turpin may not have deemed himself the most compassionate husband in Christendom, but he hoped he was far from the cruellest too.

Turpin watched as a veritable procession of street performers – acrobats, jugglers, clowns, puppeteers, musicians and, given his flute and basket, a snake charmer – worked their way through the throng, no doubt heading towards the nearest park. When he was a boy, Turpin would have followed the performers. Partly to be entertained, but more so they would have created a wonderful distraction for the thief to go about his business.

Any slither of temptation to watch the performers ply their trade was extinguished when Turpin witnessed a mime artist among the group.

He turned off the main thoroughfare, leaving the parade of shops and the colourful, chattering crowd behind. He came out into Brook Street. Turpin briefly thought, had he walked into the environs of Heaven – or another, more salubrious, circle of Hell?

Rows of large, three storey houses stood to attention, like a military guard, either side of the street. The pavements - and even the kerbs - were inordinately clean. Turpin noted that not a single window was bricked up. Due to employing lawyers and accountants to avoid various other levees, the owners could afford to pay the window tax it seemed. Many of the residents in the sought-after neighbourhood were part of the landed – lauded – gentry. Turpin thought that as grand as their townhouses were, their estates in the country would have been even grander. Money begets money. Some of the properties were fronted with spiked, iron railings – garlanded with myrtle and other flowers and plants. Footmen often stood outside the houses, discouraging riffraff from loitering – and dissuading the criminal classes from targeting the residents. Beggars, bawds and other undesirables (including swathes of the middling sort) were absent from the scene.

A ceruse-laden lady, with a thin waist and even thinner smile, walked past Turpin. She was taking her dog for its early evening constitutional, as much as it looked more like a large rat than dog. It was the latest fashionable breed, as costly to buy as a horse. The dog had just been bathed by one of the servants. In order not to besmirch its fluffy coat the owner ordered one of her footmen to carry the precious animal.

Even if Turpin would have been unfamiliar with Marie's address, he could have easily discerned which house in the street was hosting a party. Couples in their finery alighted from private coaches. To pull up in a hackney carriage would have been an embarrassment, tantamount to a venal - or cardinal - sin. Turpin suspected that some of the guests may have only lived around the corner, or even in Brook Street, but still they turned up in their elegant and expensive carriages and phaetons. Guests, in spotless frock coats and gleaming leather boots, were accompanied by their wives, or their mistresses. The butcher's son, for a moment or two, felt a little deficient. He felt that his boots were somehow not clean enough, his sword not sharp enough and face not shaven enough. He was also turning up alone, on foot. Turpin had been tempted to pay a courtesan to accompany him to the event, partly to make Marie feel a twinge of jealousy, but thought better of it.

A queue began to form on the short flight of marble stairs leading up to the house. Despite the large double doors, one woman - wearing a mighty edifice of a hooped-skirt, the shape of which seemed to defy the rules of Euclid – had to carefully manoeuvre her way through the entrance.

Turpin found himself standing next to a slight, haughty-looking gentleman, as he tarried on the stairs. He was a lord, or the son of a lord. A lifetime of being told that he was superior to others meant that the message sunk in - and he believed it with the conviction of an evangelist. Blood lines were of tantamount importance to the ruling classes, as well as to horse breeders. The gentleman wore more make-up than many of the female guests. His clothes seem to fit as tightly as a corset. Turpin's eyes ached - as if he were staring at the sun - as the outlaw glimpsed the man's silver buckles, bright and sizeable enough to serve as a mirror for the English Narcissus. He wore an overly powdered wig. More than one guest at the party, in proximity of the self-regarding aristocrat, would sneeze during the evening. The gentleman tutted in response to the inconvenience at having to wait. Turpin covertly appraised the small, emerald encrusted gold box as a distinguished guest partook of some snuff. The highwayman offered the man a polite smile, as they caught one another's eye. The aristocrat compressed his bloodless lips, rolled his eyes and offered up an askance expression in return. "Courtesy can be afforded by rich and poor alike," Turpin's mother had taught her son. The butcher's son balled his hand into a fist – and for a second or two he was tempted to knock the peacock on his arse. There would be greater profit in robbing the popinjay and his ilk, however, Turpin judged, as he smiled to himself. The fox was about to be let into the henhouse.

10.

Turpin had never particularly enjoyed the taste of champagne, but he immediately gulped down the glass, which was handed to him, as he walked out into the garden. He was keen to drown out the nagging voice of envy, which seemed to be screaming in his ear like an opera singer, as he observed Hervey and Marie playing host and hostess at the gathering. They were akin to a married couple, but happy. They stood on either side of the manicured lawn, greeting their esteemed guests.

The oblong garden – Turpin thought it shaped like a coffin – reached far back. A string quartet on a painted wooden platform sat at the other end, although he could barely hear the melodious music over the bleating guests, the chime of laughter and clinking glasses. It was all very civilised. Smartly attired waiters and waitresses weaved their way through the bejewelled party, carrying silver trays laden with full or empty glasses. Turpin would hear the word "exquisite" more than a dozen times throughout the event. The lawn was bordered by a multitude of flowers – hyacinths, magnolias, tulips and roses. The sea of green was also broken-up by narrow pathways of polished Carrara marble. The garden hosted a couple of young pear trees – and was populated by a number of stone statues (Turpin recognised the figures of Bacchus, Alexander the Great and Artemis, among others). Several figures among the guests at the ever-swelling party also caught the highwayman's eye. There was perhaps no place on the planet, at present, which rustled with as much silk, Turpin fancied. A team of pickpockets could likely retire from the potential haul on display, he calculated. Bulging wallets, handkerchiefs, pocket watchers, precious stones as populous as pebbles on a beach, were ripe for plucking, like the fruit hanging from the pear trees. A couple of barrel-chested footmen stood at the entrance to the garden, but they seemed too busy leering at the serving girls and their dresses, with pronounced low necklines, to notice anything else going on.

The footmen – and plenty of guests – also feasted on the sight of the hostess. Marie's fringe of blonde hair was curled, in the latest French fashion. Her dress was an unusual cut, the lines both accentuated her waist yet exaggerated her normally pert posterior. Purple. Pleated silk. Fine, lacework finished off the cuffs and hem. Marie was making a statement that she no longer wanted to follow the most recent fashions - but set them. A diamond necklace hung around her elegant porcelain throat, yet still her eyes shone brighter than the twinkling gem stones. Marie was mindful of staying on the marble pathways, lest her stiletto-like heels pierce and lodge in the lawn. The former artist's model appeared like she might stay eternally beautiful in life – and not just in the portraits she graced. She beamed – and not a solitary (male) guest failed to smile in reply. Men bathed in her attention like soaking up the rays of the sun. The actress remembered the names of everyone she had once met. In relation to strangers, she asked their names and how they were. Her fingertips would sometimes graze arms. Lipstick would sometimes stain cheeks, when kisses were pressed upon skin that little bit more firmly and intimately. The laughter, in response to stale witticisms, always seemed fresh. For ten to twelve seconds each, as she welcomed them to the party, people felt like they were the centre of her world. "You are Titania, Portia, and Beatrice combined," Turpin had once said to his lover, complimenting her on her charms – conveniently removing Cleopatra and Lady Macbeth from the list.

In between greeting her guests, Marie glanced over at Hervey with a look infused with ardency and devotion. Turpin suspected that she had never gazed at him in a similar fashion. Perhaps if he could have installed Marie in a house in Brook Street she might have. It was cynical but true, he thought. As most things are.

The highwayman surveyed the aristocrat, after downing another glass of champagne. Hervey was, annoyingly, handsome. *The Gentleman's Magazine* listed the bachelor as one of the most stylish figures in London society, as Hervey knew that taste was about restraint, not excess. He was equally decent and convivial company. Turpin had met Hervey at a previous party and chatted to him, before the aristocrat became his rival. He was informed, warm and self-deprecating, putting the commoner at ease at the rarefied gathering. The two men spoke about cricket, porter, guns and *Gulliver's Travels*. Hervey showed his knowledge and love of Swift's satirical work by quoting from it:

"Every man desires to live long, but no man wishes to be old."

More annoying than anything else, Turpin considered, was that Hervey made her happy, far more than the outlaw caused his own wife to be content.

As Turpin pretended not to notice Marie, Hervey only offered clandestine looks in his rival's direction, narrowing his eyes in scrutiny or displeasure. Marie had been candid and mentioned that she would invite her "friend" John Palmer. Despite having once enjoyed his company, the aristocrat wished that the lowly owner of a butcher's shop would not wish to attend. Hervey had been tempted recently to employ someone to find out more about Marie's friend, from her old neighbourhood. Perhaps he would be willing to accept a bribe to leave the couple to occupy the stage alone. Or better still, Palmer may be harbouring a past, that Hervey could leverage to his advantage. The gentleman would, at present, not lower himself to bribery or blackmail. But everyone has their price – and everyone has their secrets.

Pierre Vergier knew that the polite thing to do would be to cover his mouth with his hand when yawning – but he also wanted to advertise to the world, or party, that he was bored. That the height of sophisticated London society felt parochial to the Frenchman. The women on show wore too much perfume and make-up, or not enough. The champagne they were serving would have been labelled swill, if served at Versailles, he mused. The caterers had arranged some French delicacies, but they had anglicised them. Ruined them. The hosts had doubtless intended to imitate his countrymen, but the attempt to flatter was more of an insult to French cuisine.

The former officer scratched a speck of mud from the ornate silver pommel on his sword. He then stared at his hostess again. She may have been mindful of the latest French fashions, but Vergier judged that the low-born actress lacked a true sense of Parisian style and grace. He remembered the advice which he once gave his young cousin, in relation to courting various low-born chattel:

"Fuck them, but do not fall for them, Louis."

Granted the English woman was attractive. Granted she was not without a modicum of charm. But Hervey was debasing his family name by endeavouring to introduce the woman into civilised society. Whores should remain in the bed chamber. The actress was not even worth fathering a bastard with. Vergier had exchanged a few words with his hostess upon entering the party.

"I shall look forward to hearing the latest gossip from Paris... You have displayed a mastery of English. I hope I can call upon you later, Pierre, to make a display of your mastery over the sword. I have an actor friend attending the party who wishes to test his fencing skills."

Vergier issued a few stock compliments whilst conversing with the woman, who seemed to suffer from a need to impress or overcompensate for her lack of breeding. He smiled politely, nodded and bowed – but stopped short of embracing a commitment to take part in any exhibition of swordplay. He would not be treated like some performing monkey. The Frenchman was justly too proud to serve as a distraction or source of amusement. But there were few things Vergier enjoyed more, aside from killing and sex, than teaching a lesson to an Englishman with a sword in his hand. Attending the party had already proved worthwhile, however. The assassin could now put a face to the name - of the man he had been instructed to murder.

Turpin walked out onto the lawn and into the throng, avoiding greeting both hosts, as if negotiating a path between Scylla and Charybdis. He understandably wanted to avoid any awkwardness with Marie. Equally, he wished to evade Hervey, for different reasons. Turpin did not want to experience the scene of being treated by his hostess as if he were just another guest. The highwayman was putting on enough of an act already. Despite, or because of, the number of people around him, Turpin felt acutely lonely and isolated. He again regretted his decision not to have arranged for a courtesan to accompany him to the party.

The outlaw was drawn towards the far end of the garden, away from Marie – and close to the long table of steaming, aromatic food. He realised how hungry he was, seeing some of the dishes laid out in front of him. Gill would have salivated, in response to such a sight. There was an array of cheeses (from Europe, rather than England) on one table. Lobster. Spiced eel. Rosemary infused lamb. Salmon "from Newcastle". Buttered asparagus. Stuffed tench. Chicken livers, in a garlic sauce. Dressed crab. Honey-glazed ham.

Turpin took care not to wolf his plate down, or spill anything down his best apparel. John Palmer was a gentleman - or tried to be. He gave into further temptation as an array of pretty serving girls approached him, carrying trays of delicacies and sweets: sugared pineapple, French pasties, chocolate almonds, raspberry cream, lemon tarts, ratafia cakes. The dishes were as enticing as the figures who served them, albeit he witnessed how one of the chefs ordered one young woman, who was missing two front teeth, to keep her mouth closed and not to smile at the guests.

Unfortunately, whilst unassumingly eating and drinking away from others, Turpin was cornered by an actor, Cornelius Smythe, who had played Romeo to Marie's Juliet a year ago. Smythe, whose real name was Charles Smith, billed himself as being famous. The public would have begged to differ. The performer would have been judged handsome enough, in his prime, when wearing make-up. His eyes had grown puffy and bloodshot from drinking too much, whilst the actor was out of work, or "between productions" as he explained it. A few faded stains marked his silk shirt. His wig had seen better days. At any moment a family of insects, or a dormouse, might escape from it, Turpin imagined. Turpin also couldn't help but notice his painted-on eyebrows. The actor had shaved them off one too many times in the past – and they now refused to grow back. One hand sawed the air whilst he spoke, whilst he firmly kept hold of his glass of champagne in the other.

The thespian spoke effortlessly and effusively about himself, his past and future roles. He treated John Palmer like an audience. He was there to listen, appreciate. Smythe's voice occasionally reached a higher pitch than the violin playing in the background:

"One has to live and breathe a part. Performing is in the blood. Give me a stage. Give me excess... I was Iago, even when taking some snuff or ordering my maid to darn my stockings... Critics still rave about my Bottom... I have written a play, should you or any of your friends be interested in an investment opportunity... The title of the piece is, *He Stoops to Conquer*. It's *The Beggar's Opera* meets *Robinson Crusoe*... It cannot fail. I will of course facilitate introductions with any actresses taking part in the production."

Turpin vaguely nodded, in between mouthfuls of food and drink. He did not know whether to feel amused or weary in response to the slightly comical, slightly tragic, figure before him. When the would-be impresario realised that his audience lacked the means and vision to buy what he was selling, Smythe deftly exited the stage to seek out a more captive crowd.

Another guest soon sided up to Turpin. He was tall, but ungainly rather than elegant. Big-boned, with ample padding. He shuffled rather than strode, moving as slowly as a shire horse about to be put out to pasture. He was of a similar age to Turpin, although he looked older. Weathered. A slightly chubby face, scarred from a childhood illness, briefly scrutinised his fellow guest. His sage eyes narrowed, his thick lips were compressed together. He was far from the most sartorial figure at the gathering, but he was far from obsessive about such trivial things. Ink stained his fingers, clothes and wig. The two men recognised each other from a previous party, which Marie had invited them both to. The actress mentioned to Turpin how she wanted to stay on the right side of the writer, for fear of one day being on the wrong side of his pen:

"He can be odd, but that is why I like him. Like you, Richard, Samuel does not always fit it... I just love listening to him talk. I dare say that he is more adept at wielding words than you are at wielding a sword. Samuel is a veritable walking dictionary. I adore him."

Turpin briefly recalled what he knew of the man, from conversing with him previously and from what Marie had mentioned. He was married. From Staffordshire. Having worked as a bookbinder and schoolteacher he decided, along with his friend, David, to venture to London, "Where the streets are paved with excrement." Despite his often brooding expression the writer owned a broad sense of humour, as broad as Shakespeare's. He could be coarse, coruscating or subtly satirical with his wit. He suffered from acute bouts of involuntary tics, in regards to his hands and arms, but these subsided once he grew relaxed and comfortable in Turpin's company.

Although the learned journalist, if that wasn't a contradiction in terms, often crumpled his brow in thought, his eyes would twinkle with humour, as if the idea of life being a tragedy was just a figment of one's imagination.

"It's John, is it not? You are both a landlord and butcher, if I remember rightly? As a critic, I am paid to dissect. A man who can slaughter a pig, or pour a decent measure of ale, is worth more than any Grub Street hack, I warrant. Innkeeping is a noble profession too, far more than scribbling. There is nothing which has yet been contrived by man, by which so much happiness is produced as by a good tavern. Aye, if we consider the exchange rate further, an innkeeper is worth at least four novelists, two historians and at least six dozen adolescent poets. As prosperous as we may both be, however, we can verily be adjudged paupers in such gilded company. But you would think that, for all the capital invested in an aristocrat's education, he could afford a modicum of sympathy and imagination. I have just overheard two gentlemen talking about the poor, as if they were no better than the mud upon the soles of their shoes. "If the poor cannot raise themselves above their vices and station, then let the hole they dig for themselves serve as their grave," one of them blithely remarked, picking the lobster from their teeth. If only the poor were sufficiently wealthy, to be able to pay for such rare thinking. Poverty is a great enemy to human happiness; it certainly destroys liberty, and it makes some virtues impractical, and others impossible. A sophist may argue that all is context, or subjective. A man is only poor if he considers himself poor, they might assert. But should we not posit that there are absolutes too? Absolute truths. Moral truths. Truths by which the soul may cling to heaven, lest we plunge into hell. Or truths which prompt us to realise that compassion is a more valuable commodity than cruelty, as surely as two plus two equals four. But I fear I may be absolutely prattling on. Once a man begins to enjoy the sound of his own voice, as much as an actor, then he should cut out his tongue. Tell me, have you been faring well since we last encountered each other?"

"I can't complain. I have been faring well enough, thank you," Turpin cordially replied, his brain still trying to catch-up and store some of the words and ideas which had poured out of his companion's mouth.

"Well enough is good enough. If you are free from complaint, then you are more content than most."

Turpin nodded and smiled, as if the thought of how fortunate he was had not occurred to him before. The larder - and wine cellar - in his large house were full – and he would go home to a good wife, who was devoted to him. He knew how to tell and take a joke – and he was never short of a book to read. There were worse fates.

Samuel took a breath and mouthful of claret, as he surveyed the scene. He eyed Lord Farringdon, who had recently gone into marine insurance. He privately boasted that there was more chance of him purchasing a unicorn, than paying out on any claim. Then he noticed Sir Oswald Fry, sitting on a chair, with his left foot raised. Fry was suffering from gout, yet proud that he could afford to be so idle and rich as to contract the Disease of Kings. A footman stood by his side, holding a parasol over his head, despite the sun having long retreated behind the clouds. Ogling one of the serving girls, his eyes bulging as much as stomach, was the Marquess of Frome. "Poxy," as he was nicknamed, owned the largest collection of pornographic novels and images in London (despite the intense competition). Over the years, he had forced more than one of his teenage domestic servants to forsake the child he had fathered with them - and leave the baby at a foundling home. Perhaps one of the only decent souls present was their host, Samuel mused, although the son could afford to be innocent, given the alleged instances of butchery and larceny his father had committed during the war. Even the French did not deserve such risible treatment.

"You are certainly more content than the mass of your fellow guests. The complaints in their lives number more than the bills which arrive, to pay for the shopping trips of their wives – and mistresses. And you are doubtless more decent. Even if you left too much fat on your chops, or watered down your ale, you would still be one of the more honourable creatures currently on display here. Even I may be judged to be more honourable – and I am a journalist," Samuel remarked, permitting himself a mischievous grin. "Aye, you could even be a highwayman, John, and your crimes would be thin gruel compared to what some of our self-appointed betters are capable of. If I were any sort of critic, or man of principle, I would leave – indignant and in haste. But although I may find some of the guests here disagreeable, the food and vintages are not."

11.

The dying light was still able to seep through the threadbare curtains. Sally said that she had made the bed with her "best" sheets. If these were the best, Gill thought to himself, he would hate to see the worst. The cramped, creaking room smelled of sweat and cheap perfume. The rickety bed felt like it could fall through the rotten floorboards at any moment, and land on the patrons of the tavern below. But most were inebriated - they would barely notice.

Gill was caught between the need to catch his breath and to quench his thirst. He didn't quite achieve either, as he leaned across the bed, took a swig of ale and proceeded to spill most of the tepid drink down his chin, spluttering as he did so.

The pair lay in bed together, just holding one another, for some time. Heartbeats and breathing synchronised. Gill was tired, but contented, having travelled into the capital. He crossed over a congested London Bridge on foot and walked into *The Silver Buckle*, which doubled-up as a brothel. He ordered a drink and asked when Sally would be next free. Other girls were offered up, but Gill tied a knot in his lust while he waited.

"Will you be staying the night?" Sally asked, surprised by how much she wanted the answer to be yes – and not just due to the extra money she would earn.

"The bulge in my pocket is not just due to my full purse," Gill replied, grinning suggestively.

Sally liked the regular, who she saw at least once a month. He was fun, he never quibbled over any payment and was far more courteous than any so-called "gentlemen" who crossed over the river to see how the other side lived.

Thick, red tresses hung over milky skin. Her green eyes were wide and bright, as if she had applied belladonna to her pupils.

The girl from Cork had travelled to London with her father and brother a couple of years ago, during harvest season. She originally worked as a fruit picker in Kent. Her father worked as a labourer, but an accident caused him to injure his back. He turned to drink (even more) to quell the pain - and died within six months. Her brother returned to Ireland, but Sally knew there were few prospects back home. She moved to London and worked as a seamstress, before turning to prostitution for extra money. Originally, Sally worked out of bawd houses just off the Strand, but a couple of bad experiences prompted her to work out of a brothel. She had done her best to save some money over the past year or so, despite occasionally spending too much money on new clothes. Sally Murphy dreamed of meeting a gentleman and marrying well. She was still young enough, still pretty enough, to turn the heads of plenty of men at the Spring Gardens in Vauxhall. She worked on speaking "proper" and smoothing the rough edges of her accent, as well as improving her manners. Although Gill was no "gentleman," he was monied. She wondered if he was married. He had said no, but men were not beyond lying. Lying seemed to be their second or third favourite vice, behind drinking and tupping. Nathaniel said that he worked in a butcher's shop in Essex. She half-believed him, at best. As young as Sally was, she was not born yesterday.

"I'll give you a discount," she remarked, which was as great a token of affection as any whore could offer, plunging her hand beneath the bedsheet.

"And I'll give you a large tip as a thank you," Gill countered, his smirk as broad as his shoulders.

Turpin and Samuel spoke some more but then the latter explained that he had to take his leave:

"I should be getting back to my wife. I also have more than one article to finish. I am determined to live by my pen, even if it kills me. Thank you for making my evening more than tolerable, John. I will hopefully encounter you again soon. I must now find Marie and thank her. She is a fine woman. She knows where she is going, without wholly forgetting where she has come from. Marie has doubtless been repeatedly told how fortunate she is to be coupled with our host, but I would argue that William is the fortunate one."

The garden was now home to a veritable thicket of people. Jowls wobbled with laughter. The volume of incessant chatter increased, as guests competed to be heard. Drinks slipped down the throat, as easily as the oysters. Some form of a minor commotion seemed to be unfolding at the opposite end of the lawn. A few gasps, cheers and moments of applause sounded out. Turpin did not take much notice, however, distracted as he was by the conversation, between two of the host's friends, close by:

"Life is not about how much money one has, but how much one can borrow... His wife has apparently slept with every male member of the family, aside from her husband... As much as he could afford his South Sea Bubble losses, the wagers he has made at *White's* are costing him his house in London. I heard he lost fifty pounds the other evening, on the toss of a coin... His wife has still to recover her figure, from having the baby. She is gorging, rather than glowing... I understand that William will be leaving London tomorrow afternoon, to travel to his Norfolk estate. He is kindly giving me the use of his apartment while he is away. I will be moving in, the day after tomorrow. Marie will be accompanying him. She has landed on her feet with William, not a position she is familiar with, preferring to lie down, if the rumours are true. It is becoming her fulltime job, acting as our friend's chatelaine. 'Tis the role of a lifetime. He confessed how he may even marry the whore. Let him do as he please. Whatever makes him happy. I would just like to be present when he gives his parents the news. It's difficult to know whether his father will drop dead from shock, or shame."

Turpin was tempted to draw his sword against the young, pimply aristocrats for defaming Marie – and as much he might have liked to have robbed them the thought of burgling Hervey's apartment grew forefront in his mind. The thief might even have believed in providence. The timing was perfect. It was too good a prospect to turn down. Gill would be in town too, to assist in the robbery (and carry off more loot). Hervey had stolen Marie from him. He had every right to steal any and everything from his rival in return. The highwayman felt a little uncomfortable committing a crime against someone he knew and formerly liked, but not uncomfortable enough to prevent him from dismissing the idea. The housebreaking would be a marriage of business and personal pleasure. It was the only happy marriage that Turpin could imagine.

Tobacco smoke poured in the window, from patrons enjoying a pipe or two in the courtyard at the rear of the establishment. Kean snored, as loudly as any prize pig. Sally had worn the customer out. But he was still happily paying for her time. She moved a few strands of damp hair out of her eyes, tucked her knees up beneath the bedsheet and found herself gazing at the man next to her. The prostitute had played the part, on more than one occasion, of a victim. Pity, as well as lust, could provide a wellspring of coin. She liked to make men believe that she needed saving. That she needed funding. Sally flirted with the idea, however, that Nathaniel could be the one to genuinely save her. Meeting and marrying a gentleman was just a fanciful dream. But marrying him would not turn into a nightmare, she sensed. Sally pictured some of her careworn work colleagues. She had no desire to be plying her trade, for diminishing returns, in ten years' time. The young woman believed that she had found – and plucked out - her first grey hair yesterday morning. Why shouldn't she get to know him, outside the bedroom? Why shouldn't she allow him to take her to the park, or shopping, or for a meal? Why shouldn't she be courted, like a lady? She would not even charge him for the pleasure. Perhaps that was the clearest sign that she genuinely liked him, Sally thought. The young woman did not mind his crooked teeth, bawdy humour, rough manners – or snoring even.

The Frenchman had yet to break sweat during the display. Two bouts. Two victories. Practise swords, blunt and buttoned, had been retrieved to prevent any serious injuries. But the hits had been palpable – and the hits had hurt. First up had been the over-confident actor, Charles Murray. He had swished his sword around prettily with various practise strokes. Over the past year he had gained notable praise whilst playing the roles of Macduff and Edgar. Vergier made a fool of him - when the actor was not making a fool him himself. Murray screamed like a girl when Vergier lunged and purposely aimed for the parts of his body which were less protected and more sensitive. The thespian, who often supported political causes and had attended Cambridge for a year, only liked it when people laughed at him whilst playing comedic roles. Despite boasting beforehand to his mistress that he would teach the Frenchman a lesson, it was the Englishman who had been heavily, painfully, schooled. Murray could not quite fathom how he had failed so miserably, when every night as Macduff he had out-fenced Macbeth, and every night as Edgar he had defeated Edmund.

Next up, to challenge the "insufferable Frenchman," had been Rupert Crowne, the second son of the Duke of Suffolk. The young man toiled diligently in his pursuit of a life of leisure. He had travelled extensively in eastern Europe, bringing back all manner of Ottoman artworks and different strains of venereal disease. Crowne regularly gambled and hunted – and had retained a fencing master in his retinue for the past year or so. The gentleman easily bested his servants, who he instructed to fence with him when more able combatants were unavailable. His fencing master judged him to be one of the finest students he had ever had the pleasure to teach. "You are a natural," the tutor exclaimed, as sincerely as any actor. Before the contest, Crowne had removed his wig, lest it obstruct his view. He borrowed some suitable footwear from a friend. He complained that the practise sword was not as well-balanced as his own blade, but that it would suffice. The gentleman of leisure appeared to mean business.

Vergier tapped his foot, in mild frustration, whilst waiting for his opponent to prepare himself. The Frenchman tolerated another glass of the champagne. The Englishman offered up a procession of French phrases – *Attaque au Fer, Salut des armes, Trompement* – as he drilled himself before commencing the bout, perhaps hoping to impress or intimidate Vergier. The more Crowne puffed himself up, Vergier judged, the more he would burst the fool's bubble.

The watching crowd held its collective breath as the fencing match began. But they did not hold their breath for too long. Before one could say "parry and thrust" the Frenchman registered a clear hit, deliberately striking the buttoned end of his sword against the Englishman's nipple area. Crowne let out a curse and stamped his foot on the ground, like a spoilt child, throwing a tantrum. Vergier graciously agreed to a second contest - but duly dispatched his opponent just as swiftly again.

Crowne changed tack to then rub his shoulder – and claimed that he was suffering from an injury he had picked-up during a vigorous hunt. Few were paying much attention to the defeated second son, though. The party was focussed on Vergier. A couple of women wrote their address on a piece of paper and handed it to the Frenchman's valet, to pass on to his master.

Marie, observing the success of the entertainment she had arranged, pleaded with the Frenchman to put on one last exhibition of swordsmanship, before taking his leave. Volunteers, wary of either being humiliated or injured, were in short supply. However, the hostess knew one guest who she could compel to challenge Vergier – even though she believed that he would likely suffer humiliation and injury.

The crowd parted, allowing the actress to approach Turpin, her heels sounding upon the marble path. One couple could be heard mentioning that the stranger was one of "her friends… He has the distinct whiff of a commoner about him". Another tartly commented that, "He looks like a stagehand, who has stolen a costume from a show for the evening." Marie smiled at Turpin with whitened teeth and uncommon affection. Or common affection as he deemed it, as she had smiled at others in a similar fashion throughout the party. He half-smiled back. He told himself to be stoical, that he should put figurative wax in his ears, like sailors or yore, to avoid her siren song. He certainly had it in him to disappoint a woman. He disappointed his wife all of the time, Turpin glibly or glumly thought. The highwayman knew what Marie wanted, before she spoke. Had she invited him just to be part of the entertainment? Was he little more than a source of amusement to the capricious actress?

"John, I must call upon you to be England's champion. I will not permit you to say no," Marie said, lifting the hem up of her silk dress as she glided towards him. She fingered the pendant around her neck, directing his attention to the top of her heaving breasts. He smelled her perfume, entering his nostrils like a siren song entering his ears. Unlike the actress, Turpin felt distinctly uncomfortable at having an audience gawp at him - waiting for him to deliver his lines.

Sally, subtly or otherwise, mentioned how she was intending to visit the Spring Gardens the following day. She had arranged to see the attraction with a girlfriend of hers, who now couldn't attend. She still would dearly love to go, however. Sally then asked Nathaniel if he had ever visited the gardens.

"Yes, but I would be happy to go again. I can be free, if you would like me to come along with you?"

"I would love to spend the afternoon with you," the whore remarked, her eyes as bright as a Spring morning.

It was difficult for Gill to utter anything in reply, as Sally stopped his mouth with a luscious, lingering kiss.

Servants held lanterns aloft, along the fringe of the lawn, to illuminate the scene. Insects congregated around the lights, as several guests still congregated around the buffet tables.

Pierre Vergier apprised the women around him. He would return home soon. The question was, would he return home alone? More than one woman – wife or mistress – had offered him a telling look throughout the evening. Many of the creatures, despite their best intentions and cosmetics, were not to the Frenchman's taste, though. They were too old. Too dry. He flirted with the idea of having Gaspard pay a couple of the more comely-looking serving girls to join him back at the apartment. But young blooms can be as disease-ridden as old ones. Vergier also reminded himself that he was in attendance because he had a mission, or contract, to fulfil. Within a couple of days' time,

William Hervey, the firstborn of the Sir Edward Hervey, would be dead. The plan was to intercept the English aristocrat's coach as he travelled to his estate in Norfolk. His death would be blamed on the highwayman, Dick Turpin. Vergier had arranged to be clad in black - and ride a black mare. He would leave his whore alive, to recount the horrific crime. Vergier had given his word to the Vicomte de Montbard that he would assassinate the Englishman. He had also been paid. The French aristocrat had recently uncovered evidence that Edward Hervey was responsible for the death of his son, as the officer issued the order for every soul to be murdered during the pillaging of one of the French nobleman's estates. The massacre had occurred decades ago, during the War of Spanish Succession, but the wound was still tender, as if inflicted yesterday. The vicomte would exact his revenge – an eye for an eye – by butchering Hervey's firstborn. "He deserves to experience the same grief and grievance I suffered," he had told Vergier, spitting the words out like a snake emitting venom. The famed highwayman would take the blame for the murder. Should he be apprehended and deny the crime, no one would believe that the outlaw was innocent.

Vergier did not think much of his final opponent. The Englishman was doubtless wearing his best attire, but his clothes were not quite fine enough, the Frenchman judged. His hair was too lank, his face not clean-shaven enough. Something was not quite right with the stranger. Something was out of place, like topping off an outfit with the wrong hat. Vergier had served as a spy. He trusted his instincts when it came to deceiving - or judging that he was being deceived. Was the new competitor a plant, invited by the hostess to embarrass the Frenchman? Vergier remained imperious, impervious. The agent had trained himself to observe, rather than react to, events.

If the bastard fences as well as his dresses, then I am in trouble, Turpin half-joked to himself as he apprised his opponent.

"Pierre, I would like to introduce you to John Palmer, an old and dear acquaintance of mine."

The two men shook hands. Vergier noted how rough the Englishman's palm was. He was a fish out of water.

He is no gentleman.

"I hope you acquit yourself better than your predecessors," Vergier remarked, not without a sly smile.

"I dare say that I cannot do any worse," Turpin replied, impressed by the Frenchman's faultless accent. He could almost pass as a native. As seriously as

Turpin would take the contest, the Englishman believed that there was always space for a slither of dry humour in any situation.

"Indeed," Vergier countered, humourlessly, whilst smoothing out one of his eyebrows.

"I was hoping that you might even take pity on me and spare my blushes," Turpin said, as he removed his jacket in preparation. He observed a few gentlemen in the crowd begin to make wagers on the match. Should Gill have been present, he would have asked his friend to put some money on him, once the odds grew long enough.

"No matter how much wealth I accumulate, I find I can never afford to spare pity. Mercy is the malady of the weak. I assume that you are not a nobleman," Vergier uttered, with a certain measure of disdain etched into features, like words chiselled into a gravestone.

"No. I am something slightly better than a nobleman. An Englishman," Turpin responded. A hint of belligerence now flavoured his good-humoured tone. The outlaw did not particularly need an excuse to dislike the French aristocrat, but he was being furnished with one or two nonetheless.

The self-proclaimed Englishman in front of him would suffer the same fate as the limp-wristed actor and over-confident dandy, Vergier deemed.

Even if he proves a superior swordsman to his countrymen, he will still not be able enough. The English are renowned for their crapulence, not competence.

Turpin regretted drinking too much champagne. He would have also preferred to see the Frenchmen fence beforehand, to assess his strengths and style.

Marie stood in between the competitors and said a few words, before commencing the fencing match. The actress was not averse to being the centre of attention. Hervey watched from the side lines, seemingly indifferent. On the one hand he was keen for his rival to be humiliated, but on the other he was keen for the arrogant Frenchman to chalk up a loss. If only they could both lose. He diplomatically refrained from placing a bet on either competitor, although he estimated that Palmer had scant chance of besting the skilled Frenchman.

The two men nodded at one another to signal their readiness. Both subtly smiled too. Turpin did so, wryly thinking that the French aristocrat had no idea that he was about to fence against an infamous outlaw. A common criminal. Vergier smirked in return, knowingly and scornfully, judging that the Englishman was ignorant of his opponent. The assassin had killed countless men, during duels or more dishonourable encounters. He could similarly dispatch his fellow party guest, without remorse, in the blink of an eye. He was tempted to injure the insolent Englishman more severely than his previous opponents (he possessed the skill to make it appear like an accident), but Vergier was mindful of not wanting to draw too much attention to himself or be the subject of any unwanted interest or gossip.

Unlike Vergier's two previous opponents, Turpin did not immediately and impulsively lunge forward and attack. He parried, and then parried again. The two men felt each other out, like two pugilists might jab from a distance, not really concerned about landing a decisive blow. Blades clinked together, like tankards toasting one another. A few gasps scratched the air when Turpin briefly lost his footing, slipping on a patch of wet grass. Vergier refrained from taking advantage. He was keen to win by fair, rather than foul, means. Marie gasped a little louder than the rest of the party, drawing attention to herself (or she may have been genuinely worried for her old friend). A couple of other ladies proceeded to mimic the reactions of their hostess.

The crowd edged backwards, allowing the competitors more room to engage one another. The Frenchman displayed the more elegant style and graceful footwork. Turpin soon admitted to himself that his opponent was the superior swordsman. But that did not equate to certain defeat. The determined Englishman would turn weakness into strength – and turn the Frenchman's confidence into over-confidence. He would feign difficulty and then counter-attack.

Vergier believed he had the beating of the Englishman. He would win, through his ability and sheer force of will. It was also the natural order of things that the nobleman should best the commoner. There was tacit agreement that the system of selective breeding worked, in relation to horses, livestock and hunting dogs. Selective breeding, through the comingling of the nobility, worked as a system to improve society too, the aristocrat believed, with an almost religious conviction.

Beads of sweat appeared on the Englishman's brow. His expression betrayed flecks of distress. He moved backwards, barely remaining on the edge of the lawn. The crowd sensed that at any moment the Frenchman would finish off his opponent, after toying with him.

Turpin hoped he had inspired a sense of complacency, as well as triumph, in the Frenchman. With renewed speed and directness, he parried and thrust his buttoned blade forward. For a brief moment it was Vergier's expression that exhibited distress. But it was all too brief. The experienced swordsman turned his body out of the way in time – whilst punching his own weapon forward.

"A hit!" one of the spectators announced – or ejaculated.

The butcher's son felt a sharp pain in his ribs – and was on the cusp of launching into a stream of curses, which would have sounded more at home in the environs of a street market in Southwark, as opposed to a garden party in Brook St. But he glimpsed at his hostess and desisted, for fear of embarrassing her.

The self-satisfied, or goading, smile on the Frenchman's face gleamed like a polished cutlass. Both opponents offered each other a perfunctory, sporting nod.

"Do not feel too disconsolate. You fought well. Should I have the time later I may be able to provide some pointers, for you to refine your stance and style," the aristocrat remarked, not a little patronisingly.

Turpin forced a smile and polite comment in reply, through gritted teeth. If he gripped his sword any tighter, he would have developed a blister. He felt that he had somehow let himself, Marie and even England down by losing to the conceited foreigner. He felt like being sick, like he had downed a pint of bile. The outlaw felt like he had been robbed. The defeat would leave a temporary bruise on his ribs, but the loss would injure his pride for much longer.

A gloom descended, despite more lamps being lit. A gaggle of enamoured women - and a few enamoured men - flocked towards the victor. Congratulating him. Cooing over him. Vergier graciously received their compliments, but largely detested them. Not a single guest present would be deserving of inhabiting the hallowed court of Versailles, he haughtily imagined.

The champagne continued to flow. Now that the entertainment had ceased, guests continued their conversations, clustering together like flies around a carcass, gossiping about those in their set who were absent from the party. Caesar had fewer knives in his back. Turpin cut a lone, forlorn figure - too exhausted, or embittered, to drown his sorrows. Marie veered off towards Hervey after the defeat, not caring to offer some words of consolation to her friend. John Palmer was a leper, in more ways than one. When Turpin heard Marie let out a laugh, in response to something Hervey said, it hurt more than the pain in his ribs. He took a seat and bowed his head, in shame or despondency. Or both. The outlaw didn't belong. The food was too rich, the company too galling and deluded. He realised that he wanted to be home. Not in St Giles, but in Buckhurst Hill. He preferred Elizabeth's cooking to the delicacies on display. He wanted to laugh and share a jug of ale with Gill, instead of listen to a fellow guest boast about how many acres he owned, and how much the value of his townhouse in London had increased recently.

But all was far from lost. The party would not be a complete waste of time, or a lesson in abject failure. Turpin's ears pricked up – and his spirits lifted – when he overheard a conversation between Vergier and his valet. Finally, learning the French language was bearing some fruit. Vergier mentioned that they should soon leave the party. There was still much to arrange, regarding their trip the following day. Their apartment would be vacant tomorrow evening.

Turpin neither possessed the time or will to say goodbye to the host and hostess – and thank them for an exquisite evening. Instead, he was more concerned with stealing a glance in Marie's address book on the way out, which contained the names and addresses of attendees. He was intending to steal a lot more. The Frenchman may well possess valuables that even Colman would pay a fair price for, the highwayman thought. Breaking into Hervey's property could wait. There was mettle even more attractive. Turpin may have lost a battle this evening, against Vergier, but he was determined to win the war.

12.

Rain thrummed against the window. A couple old, Irish sots, slurring their speech, retched in the alley below. A cat's tail knocked over a bottle and smashed it, as it pursued a charcoal-coloured rat. Turpin could smell the landlord's wife cooking, unfortunately.

Despite the copious amounts of brandy he consumed when he returned to his lodgings in Cockspur Street, Turpin still couldn't wash away the bitter taste of defeat in his mouth. He had given it his all against the Frenchman, but his best still hadn't been good enough. The foreigner had out-fenced him.

Turpin found himself admitting defeat when it came to winning the prize of Marie too. Second-best was also last place. If Marie had not made her choice already, she would soon, he imagined. The butcher's son felt like he possessed lead in his soul, and Hervey possessed gold. Perhaps it was for the best. Had he not loved the idea of Marie more than the reality? The actress had developed expensive tastes over the years. It should have come as no surprise to the highwayman that she would want to chew him up and spit him out. Turpin recalled some lines from Hamlet:

"She would hang on him as if increase of appetite would grow by what it fed on."

He had hung on her, he realised. But he no longer felt that increase of appetite and growth. If love is a sickness, he may have been cured, Turpin fancied. Or was he, like almost everyone else, deluding himself? A shard of bitterness still gnawed his innards, growing by what it fed on.

Turpin peered up at the ceiling, with bruise-coloured eyelids. A spider was spinning a web, from a rusty lamp which hung down. Turpin asked himself, his breath stained with brandy, if he was a spider, creating a web, or merely a fly, fated to be caught in one?

Turpin arrived at the *The Silver Buckle* around noon the following day. He purchased a couple of laundry bags on the way, to carry any prospective loot. Gill knew a hackney carriage driver, Daniel Grey, who would be able to take them to and from the scene of the crime. The only question Grey would ask would be, how much am I getting paid? Turpin intended to scout out the street and property later that afternoon, before entering under the cover of darkness. It may be the only crime that he would ever be forgiven for by the English authorities – that of robbing a French aristocrat.

During the morning he had sat in a coffee shop with a blank sheet of paper in front of him, as seemingly empty as his heart, torn over the letter to write to Marie. Should he just politely thank her for the party? Should he come across as wistful or wounded? Should he end the affair, before she could? Part of him wanted to make her feel guilty. Punish her in some way. But not punish her too much. In the end, the page remained blank. He had little idea when any missive would reach her too. She was travelling with Hervey today, to his house in a genteel part of Essex. They would then proceed to his estate in Norfolk. The family possessed as many properties as fingers – and toes.

As Turpin finished his coffee, he resolved that the next time that Marie spotted him in the audience, he would be sat beside another mistress (younger and prettier than the actress). The highwayman was pleased, though, by how easily his thoughts turned from Marie to the new job at hand.

The beetle-browed proprietor of the *The Silver Buckle*, Saul Romney, mentioned that Gill was out, with not a little disgruntlement, when Turpin asked after his friend. Not only was Romney peeved that one of his best girls was not available to work, but to add insult to injury she had taken one of her best customers away for the day. If the stout Gill was here right now, he would have been on his second jug, at least, and third course.

Romney replied that Gill would be back soon, hoping that his companion might then remain in the tavern and spend some money, to compensate him for the big drinker's absence.

Turpin decided to wait. He sat on a table in the corner, pulled his hat down and collar up, to lessen the odds of anyone recognising him, and worked his way through a measure of porter.

"Would you like a woman, to keep you company and pass the time?" Romney asked, scratching a blotchy rash on his neck. The proprietor was always mindful of squeezing out extra revenue, as he was of making sure every drop of drink from a bottle or barrel was used.

"No, I'm miserable enough already," Turpin drily replied.

It was a fine day. The rain during the night had cleared the air. The Spring Gardens, in summer, were in bloom. Ubiquitous, but nevertheless pretty, elm trees provided a vernal canopy over the paths which people blithely strolled along. The lower ranks donned their best apparel. Some were mindful not to drop their aitches – and add their tees and gees. The middling ranks did not altogether know if they should consider themselves their betters. Hats were tipped. Smiles were offered up freely, although some folk were justly conscious of concealing their less than pristine teeth. A string quartet played upon the freshly painted bandstand. Visitors milled upon and around the Chinese pavilion, wearing a range of colours to rival the flowerbeds. Other small groups congregated around a recently erected statue of Handel, or the newly installed pieces of art being exhibited. Advertisement boards, for cosmetics and dress shops, caught the eye. Promising the earth. Costing it too. Solitary walkers and families all took their turns around the park. Old married couples strolled hand in hand, along with husbands and mistresses, wives and lovers. Although the gardens were home to a few thousand visitors a day, they rarely appeared overcrowded. People gave one another their space to find some rare repose in the often unpleasant capital, filled with often unpleasant souls. Jonathan Tyers, a leather maker from Bermondsey, who had regenerated the gardens and provided new attractions in 1732, was often thanked for his achievement. He warmly accepted the praise, as well as gratefully accepting the small entrance fees.

Nathaniel and Sally walked arm in arm. Neither could remember if he took her arm, or she his. But it didn't matter. They spoke about everything and nothing. Sally could not recall when she had laughed or enjoyed herself so much.

"I want to know more about you... You are not secretly married I hope, although I would still happily help you commit adultery if you were," Sally said, hoping her late Catholic mother could not hear her, as she affectionately squeezed his arm.

"Married men don't smile this much. It's nice that you could be jealous though, if I was married," Gill replied.

"Now tell the truth. I know when men are lying. It's usually when they open their mouths. Do you really work as a butcher? People who earn honest livings often don't make that much of a living."

"I have worked as a butcher in the past. But my living is not wholly honest nowadays, though I like to think it's more honest than some professions. Than politicking and preaching, for instance."

"Are you a thief?" Sally asked, more curious than condemnatory.

"No more than the taxman," he countered. "I have done some things that I'm not proud of. But who hasn't? I'm just trying to earn a living, honest or otherwise. It may be that I have to keep some secrets for you, as a husband does a wife."

"You could be Dick Turpin, for all I know!"

They both laughed, albeit for different reasons.

The mounts pulling the coach kept a good, even pace. The devil wasn't at their heels, or hooves - but better to be safe than sorry. Sunlight slanted through the window, bathing Marie's already redolent features in a healthy glow. The neck of a half-empty bottle of champagne rhythmically clinked against the rim of the silver bucket it rested in.

Hervey had arranged for some extra plump cushions to be installed in the carriage, to make the journey more comfortable for Marie. The actress sat next to Hervey, leaning her head against his arm. She was mindful of positioning her head so that she avoided catching her new diamond earrings, which Hervey had bought her, on her hair or his velvet coat. She had taken her shoes off, fearful of developing corns of her feet (and she did not have Gertrude with her to help remove them).

Her almond eyes were half-closed, in tiredness and contentment, like a purring cat. Marie still thought about Turpin, but not as much as she used to.

The actress often imagined that if the highwayman were apprehended or killed and she was revealed to be his lover – then she might become, for a time, the most famous woman in England. But the celebrated performer realised that love and money were more valuable than fame. William was the safer – and more profitable – bet. Should William ask her to marry him, she would say "yes" before he even finished asking the question. Marie pictured, again, the estate they were travelling to. She had seen a painting of the grand house, with its colonnades and extensive grounds, stretching out for as far as the eye could see. One day it could all be William's. And hers.

No dream could be as sweet as what he was experiencing now, Hervey fancied as he kissed the top of his sleeping beauty's head. He smoothed his eyebrow and dusted a couple of crumbs off his beloved jacket. He wondered if she could feel the bulge in his pocket – from the ring he intended to give her during the coming weekend at his family home. William loved her. He lived for very looks. He would die for her.

Sally felt safe with "her Nathaniel". Whether other people felt safe, when he creased his brow or hardened his glare, was another matter, she mused.

Sally grinned, as she pictured him confronting the bothersome figure in the park, earlier in the afternoon. Jerimiah Cob was dressed in black and appeared as solemn-faced and constipated as a priest. The puritan perched himself on a small crate he had brought with him – and started to extol the evils of gin:

"Do not permit Madame Geneva to seduce you… Drink equates to damnation, in this world and the next. It is a mortal sin. Your soul will be poisoned… Drinking will prove hazardous to your health," Cob continued to pontificate, irritating a myriad of passers-by – and not just because he originally from Birmingham.

"Talking about drinking will prove hazardous to your health soon, because I'll put you on your arse if you don't move along," Gill remarked, flatly. It was a promise more than a threat. As much as the campaigner felt that he had God on his side, Cob prudently decided to withdraw. The activist also told himself that he needed to attend another venue, to warn against the evils of voting Tory. If only people heeded his advice, he judged, the world would be a better place.

More than one spectator clapped, after Gill persuaded the old goat of a man, who was disturbing the peace and quiet, to hector people outside of the gardens. Sally felt strangely proud of Nathaniel, like a wife would her husband.

His stock rose too when Sally realised that her regular was sufficiently wealthy to not bat an eyelid at the extortionate prices that the food and drink vendors charged in the Spring Gardens. He bought some cakes and a quart of fruit punch, which he lamented for tasting more of fruit than alcohol.

"Tell me about your cottage, back home. Do you have any land too – and a garden?"

"Aye, I have a small portion of land. I should do more with it. The cottage could be more homely too. It needs a woman's a touch," the rough-hewn highwayman remarked, with a tender, vulnerable and suggestive look in his red-rimmed eyes.

Turpin watched, through the murky window, as a hollow-cheeked mother balanced her wailing child in one arm, whilst carrying two jugs of cloudy gin on the other, before spying Gill coming towards the tavern. He was with a young, flame-haired woman. She stood on tiptoe and kissed his visibly smitten friend on the cheek. Despite plenty of competition, it was one of the more memorable kisses he received from the woman during the past day and night. Turpin was pleased that his friend was potentially courting and making a life for himself, outside their life of crime and nights spent in *The Cockpit*.

The woman retreated, scurrying a little as if tardy, into the backrooms of the establishment. Her heart-shaped, freckled face was a picture of breathless delight. She wanted to tell her best friend about her day. About "her Nathaniel".

Saul Romney observed the scene. The sour-faced proprietor looked like he had just been forced to drink half a pint of curdled milk. His left eye twitched, whilst his right was screwed-up in perturbation. He had seen it all before. A brothel is no place for love or courtship. Sooner or later, he would have to wipe away the tears, when the girl's hopes were dashed - as well as wipe away all other manner of stains that the establishment accrued.

Turpin greeted his pleasantly surprised friend and bought him a drink. They sat in a booth, ensconced in the corner, to talk privately.

"You seem enamoured. Rosie will be jealous. You'll be picking flowers and writing poetry next," Turpin remarked, gently teasing his gently blushing companion.

"I will be ducking your head in the trough outside, that's what I'll be doing. Are you not the wrong side of the river? Did you run out of champagne where you were - and you fancied having a proper drink?" Gill replied, making sure to avoid the small pools of ale as he rested his elbows on the table.

"I'm here to tell you to stop stealing hearts. I've found something far more valuable to filch, my friend. You will need to change out of your Sunday best clothes – and wash that lipstick from your cheek. It's time to go to work."

13.

The dead of night. The late-night revellers were asleep. Even the most diligent of constables had turned in too. The once balmy air was infected with a chill. Thick, woollen clouds snuffed out the lambent moonlight. The weather, or God, was smiling on their enterprise, Turpin fancied. "Even God doesn't like the French. He's only human," he had once heard Colman remark. Lamps and lanterns had been extinguished, all along the row of town houses and apartment buildings. It had now been over an hour since the street had seen its last activity. An elegantly dressed, inebriated figure had pulled up in a phaeton, fondling a finely dressed, unrefined woman. He had probably spent the evening at his club – and worked his way home via one of the more respectable brothels. Turpin noticed a few curtains twitch as the gentleman bundled the giggling woman through the door. A married couple peered down from the second-floor window of the adjacent property. The wife scowled, the soul of disapproval. The husband appeared a picture of envy, however.

Turpin and Gill were sat in the back of a hackney carriage. A blanket covered their legs – and concealed the tools of their trade. No one paid the cab, or its passengers, any heed. For the most part they were cloaked in darkness. The two men had reconnoitred the property during the afternoon. Not only had Vergier, along with his valet, departed, but the apartment on the ground floor was vacant too. Providence was indeed smiling on them. It would be a crime not to take advantage of the opportunity before them. The housebreakers also planned their prospective escape routes and rendezvous points, should they need to flee. They cut short their drinking session afterwards. They needed to keep a clear head. A business head. Turpin imagined that the haul could prove valuable enough to fund his retirement, or at least allow him to take a break from his criminal activities for a while. No one can remain an outlaw forever. On more than one occasion of late he had rubbed his stubbled neck, imagining a noose tightening around it. He would, sooner or later, need to become John Palmer. Live an honest live. There were worse fates. But the highwayman - and the English reading public - wanted Dick Turpin to ride again.

Just before they approached the door the two men stood still, their eyes wolf-like pricked to attention, to listen for any footsteps approaching.

The cab driver, Daniel Grey, observed the spectral figures from the far end of the street. Grey yawned, scratched his groin and lit his pipe. The wizened, ornery Cornishman owned a glass eye. The rogue was willing to turn a blind eye, however, and transport the housebreakers to and from their job, so long as he received payment beforehand.

"No offence, but if you're caught then I'll be out of pocket," the hackney carriage driver remarked to his infrequent drinking companion, as they discussed their enterprise.

Grey offered up a grunt cum hum of respect as he watched the two men pass through the front door of the house swiftly and silently. He couldn't tell whether they possessed a key or jemmied it open. Not even Dick Turpin himself could break in that quickly, he mused. Grey sat next to an empty bottle on his seat, which he would proceed to smash – and alert Nat and his confederate – should anyone else enter the property. It was a service which the driver was all too willing to provide for his friend, for an additional shilling.

Anxiety and excitement chequered their hearts. Come the morning they could hold a life-changing fortune in their hands - or be incarcerated, awaiting execution. If caught they would be condemned to death. Crime could not be seen to pay. The property-owning classes also owned the oxymoron of the justice system.

Turpin and Gill ascended the stairs, with the former noting a painting on the wall worth taking on their way out. There was also the option of breaking into the ground floor apartment, should the haul from the Frenchman's residence prove disappointing. The housebreakers carried certain tools of their trade, including iron crows, hammers and chisels. Their long coats also housed a brace of pistols. More tools of their trade. Brandishing the weapons would dissuade anyone from intervening or playing the hero. Most of the shots that Turpin had fired from his pistol over the years had been warning shots. Most, but not all. He had fired a warning shot over the head of Thomas Morris, but it did not deter the man, intent of securing the bounty for capturing the notorious Dick Turpin. The second shot did end any chance of Morris earning a reward, however.

Gill used brute force to prise open the lock on the door to the apartment. Turpin first cast the room in darkness even more, by closing the curtains, before lighting a solitary lamp.

"So, are we going to hear the sound of wedding bells soon, with you and this Sally?" Turpin remarked, hoping to ease some of the eerie tension.

"I want to hear the ring of French coin first. So did this garlic muncher really best you with a sword?"

"Aye, he did. Thank you for reminding me."

"My pleasure."

"In my defence, he is regarded as one of the finest blades in France."

"It seems he should also be regarded as one of the best blades currently in England too," Gill replied, unable to suppress a good-humoured smirk.

"Touché."

Gill ventured into the master bedroom, carrying an empty laundry bag, which he hoped to fill. He wondered if the sartorial Frenchman kept any items of women's clothing in his wardrobe, left there by lovers or mistresses. He might get lucky and find something for Sally. She would have to get used to living off the proceeds of crime if they were to begin courting in earnest. All that glittered was gold enough. Gill scooped up any jewellery in the dresser drawers. He turned his nose up at the overly florid fragrances, but indiscriminately pilfered the various bottles of perfume on show. A large, ornate clock perched on solid silver feet, with a bejewelled face, also sat on the mahogany dresser. Such was its bulk and weight that he would probably need help in removing the item. If need be, Gill would extract the feet and jewels – and leave the remainder of the well-crafted timepiece in a state of disrepair. One of the housebreaker's prized finds was a golden toothbrush, which he found upon the bedside table. He marvelled at the luxury item – to the point where he was tempted to keep it, rather than sell on. But the horse may have bolted in relation to the Englishman taking good care of his teeth.

Turpin thought the décor was elegant in some instances, gaudy in others. In short, French. Although he had learned the language and enjoyed French literature, Turpin had no yearning to travel to Paris or even visit the part of Kensington which had become a veritable French ghetto. The bruise, from Vergier's buttoned sword tip, still smarted. But Turpin imagined that coming home to a burgled apartment, with many of one's prized possessions taken, would smart even more.

The housebreaker methodically pocketed a timepiece, a small bag of coins, an engraved silver snuffbox and an opal festooned brooch from the bureau by the window. Turpin also tucked a finely crafted gold letter knife, with a pearl embedded in its hilt, into his breeches. He efficiently rummaged through the various compartments of the bureau, which largely contained stationery and invoices. The thief was naturally attracted to the large drawer, which remained locked, in the piece of furniture though. There was little light in the room, but Turpin's eyes still gleamed as he broke open the drawer with a hammer and chisel.

Turpin removed the journal from the compartment, initially disappointed that he did not encounter anything of substantial value. The book fell open, as eventually did the highwayman's mouth, on the page of the last diary entry, which Vergier had composed that morning. The handwriting was small and slanted, but clear and neat. The Frenchman's penmanship, like his swordsmanship, was excellent. Exquisite. Turpin was unable to translate every word, but he understood most of what he read. And enough was enough.

"Another day. Another death. Either I may be considered an instrument of providence, hastening souls to their fate, or, should God be no more real than a dragon or nereid, then Man is the legislator for his own moral code - and all is permissible... The trap will soon be set – and soon be sprung. William Hervey must die tomorrow. Tragically, or comically, he has aided his own demise. I spoke to Hervey yesternight, at a decidedly tawdry party he hosted (both the

cuisine and the odious company of the guests left a bitter taste in one's mouth). He duly confirmed the route that his carriage will take on the way to his family's estate. I have arranged a carriage myself. We shall lie in wait on a suitably narrow stretch of the highway, with one of our wheels seemingly in a state of disrepair. Before the coachmen have a chance to suspect a ruse, I will be close enough to draw my pistols on them, leaving their passengers unguarded. Hervey will die by my blade, as I promised the Vicomte de Montbard. His whore, a base actress called Marie Harley, I will leave alive, if only to testify that the highwayman, Dick Turpin, was guilty of the crime. I will be dressed in black, masked – and in possession of a black mare, like the renowned highwayman. Should I be in the mood, I may steal what little is left of her virtue, as well as any valuables. Should the woman somehow recognise me, however, she will not live to tell anyone... It has been a month now since Montbard originally bored me, recounting his grief and crusade to uncover evidence of Edward Hervey's complicity in his son's death. If I was Montbard, I would have exacted my revenge on the merest suspicion that the English officer issued the order to murder my kin. He should be bloodying his own blade, but he has contracted out mine to expedite his revenge. His cowardice is my good fortune. I believe that he finally summoned up the will to kill the firstborn, in revenge for his own loss, not just because he found evidence of the crime. Rather, old Montbard realises that he is dying. He will only die a happy man, if he is able to compel his enemy to be as miserable as he is. Montbard also realises that time will catch up with the Englishman too. "An eye for an eye, a son for a son. I want him to die of a broken heart," the ailing aristocrat confessed to me, with a wine-stained, malicious grin. His face was as wrinkled as a walnut – dried and shrivelled-up. He bewailed his fate and unpacked his heart like whore, complaining that the death of his only son had broken his ancestral line. He should have discarded his barren wife, re-married and sired a son to maintain his blood stock. "Money is no object," he also foolishly remarked, when engaging my services. Montbard will satisfy his ire soon and find some peace, from the death of William Hervey. I will satisfy my desire to purchase another vineyard in

Burgundy. If Montbard would have asked me to – and offered a sufficient fee – I would cut out Hervey's heart and bring it back to France... It is useful to visit England every once in a while, but only to remind myself how much I revile the perfidious county. It's bovine women and sodden climate. It's vulgar culture and licentious peasantry..."

For a moment, Turpin imagined a scenario in which the Frenchman murdered Hervey – and he could comfort Marie while she grieved. His rival would ultimately become an unpleasant memory. He would have his mistress back. He would win. Marie would know that the highwayman was an impostor – and he would be guiltless of the crime. More than nigh on anyone else, Marie was intimate with the real Dick Turpin. For a moment he thought of the prospective size of the haul from the current robbery. He was confident that the property contained a strongbox of coin somewhere. Such wealth could be life changing. He could afford to establish himself as a horse trader. He could earn an honest living. He could pretend to be John Palmer, if it meant that he lived. For a moment, the outlaw thought that he could live happily ever after. And for a moment he felt like he was suspended in mid-air - as he read the disorientating words in the diary - like a condemned man on the gallows, just after the trapdoor is pulled.

Turpin's features hardened, as did his resolve. There would be no opportunity to warn the couple of the impending ambush. The outlaw could not alert the authorities. There was a fair chance that the assassin could end up targeting him, as well as Gill - but Dick Turpin would ride out at least one last time.

14.

Turpin, clutching the journal, instructed his friend to leave immediately – and just bring whatever loot he was carrying with him. There was a sharp edge to his voice, akin to an executioner's axe. Gill was slightly confounded, as he watched his friend prematurely stride out of the apartment. But he had learned to trust his confederate's instincts and judgement over the years.

"Is something wrong?" he asked, as he caught up to Turpin on the stairs.

"Yes," the highwayman simply and wanly replied, as if the world might end.

Gill was still in the dark, in more ways than one. He glanced wistfully at the valuable painting on the wall, like a half-cut drunk who could no longer afford another drink.

"There has been a change of plan. Can you take us to Whitechapel? Speed is of the essence," Turpin remarked to Grey.

"It will cost you extra."

"How much?"

Grey ruminated, chewing his lips for a few seconds, before naming what he thought was an exorbitant price, to match his passenger's apparent desperation. He was somewhat crestfallen, however, when Turpin agreed instantly to pay the sum, leaving the driver to stew in the realisation that he could have charged him more.

Turpin was still trying to comprehend events himself, as he explained things to Gill. Was he the victim of fate, or mere coincidence? Was he the spider or the fly? Perhaps his crimes were about to catch up with him. The wages of sin must be paid. Gill's eyes grew bulbous in disbelief. His expression was a patchwork of incredulity and revelation. He swore, more than usual, underneath his breath as Turpin gave an account of what he had read.

"I need to try and put myself in between Vergier and his target. I cannot ask you to do the same. I could be signing your death warrant.

I do not know the extent of the opposition I might face. If I fail, I could be painting a target on my own back for the assassin," Turpin argued.

"You do not have to ask, for me to give you an answer. I would never forgive myself, Dick, if I abandoned you now. We have faced greater odds, I suspect. And who else can I ask to be my groomsman when I get married?"

Parts of London were eerily quiet. Only a handful of haggard prostitutes populated the crossroads on the Strand. One of the drabs pulled open her shawl and flashed Gill, but thankfully the carriage was travelling too fast - and it was all a blur. Turpin could smell sulphur in his nostrils. He wondered if the gates of Hell had opened – to allow a demon out, or to welcome a soul in.

The highwayman sketched out his plan to his friend, with hope more than certainty etched in his pale features. They would look to hire a coach when they reached Whitechapel. Although there would scarce be any sober drivers available who were keen to travel at night, Turpin would offer them a fee to make the fare worthwhile. Once they reached Buckhurst Hill, they would saddle Black Bess and Turpin's second horse, Hector, for Gill to ride. They would then race to intercept Hervey on the road to Norfolk before he was ambushed by the assassin.

"It's a desperate plan, I know, but it's the only plan we have."

Shortly afterwards the two men sat in silence. In the gloom. The ruts and holes in the road jolted them awake whenever they were on the cusp of sleep. The brick buildings, once densely hanging over them like a canopy of trees, were thinning out. Turpin shifted in his seat a little, partly to avoid the point of the letter knife digging into his back. He shifted uncomfortably in his seat as well, knowing that he needed to kill again. The outlaw closed his eyes. Instead of seeing Vergier, though, the image of Thomas Morris appeared. Morris encountered Turpin by happenstance, whilst he hid out in Epping Forest after a robbery. Morris was a servant to one of Forest Keepers. He had an innocent face. Whether he had an innocent heart or not, it was difficult to tell. He was perhaps as innocent as the next man, which is no great boast. Certainly, Morris was naïve, as he recognised the renowned highwayman and believed that he could apprehend or kill Turpin on his own. Perhaps he thought himself the hero in his own story. Or Morris experienced a pang of greed, and he did not want to share the reward money with anyone else. Turpin's hideout was a small cave, in the heart of the forest, largely concealed by the dense woodland. It was furnished with bedding, victuals, wine and other provisions, including a well-thumbed copy of Hamlet. Morris was armed with a pistol and knife. He stalked his prey, knowing that he would need to close on his target to make any shot count. Bracken snapped beneath his feet, alerting Turpin to the man's presence. Morris let off a panicked shot, which flew well wide. Turpin drew two pistols and fired a warning shot - but knew he would be wasting a bullet if he returned fire again, as his assailant retreated behind the trunk of a fallen elm tree. The highwayman sped into his cave and retrieved his carbine. Morris reloaded, panting, his hands shaking with fear more than excitement - losing sight of the outlaw as he did so. Thankfully, Morris spied the point of the highwayman's cocked hat, poking out from behind a birch tree. He was caught in two minds, between stalking his prey still or racing back to muster a larger force to capture the outlaw. But the hunted became the hunter. Turpin had deliberately hung his hat, part exposed, on the tree. He proceeded to stealthily work his way around to outflank his assailant, taking care to assess if the pistol-wielding man was alone. Morris was biting his bottom lip and wiping a sweaty palm on his breeches when Turpin crept up beside him, his carbine raised and trained at his opponent's head.

"Drop the pistol on the ground," Turpin instructed, his voice and features as hard as flint. The highwayman did not wish the kill the man, but he would need to restrain him if he was to break camp and escape, without being followed. Something possessed Morris - a sense of justice or foolishness – to compel him to attack, rather than surrender. He swiftly turned and aimed his pistol. But not swiftly enough. There was no time to think about just wounding his attacker. The bullet from the carbine smashed through his chest, bursting his heart. Such was Turpin's proximity to Morris, that flecks of blood and sinew marked his face, like welts or scars. Anger and mournfulness vied for sovereignty in his being, like two dogs fighting over a bone. He cursed the dead man for his stupidity. Turpin had fought before, threatened before, tortured before, discharged his weapon before – but never killed a man. He had crossed the Rubicon. Turpin found his way home. His wife knew something was wrong - from his haunted expression and bedraggled appearance - as soon as he walked through the door. But Elizabeth never asked about where he had been, what he had done – and Turpin never told her. The body of Morris was found. Newspaper reports rightly accused Dick Turpin of murder. He was called "the butcher highwayman". Turpin preferred a previous description of the "dandy highwayman" in one of the newspapers. But the former title seemed more apt. He drank, to try and lift or drown out his spirit. But he failed to do either. Sleep was a precious, but rare, balm. He tried to scrub his skin clean, believing he could still smell the powder from the carbine. He prayed that he would never have to kill again – but his prayers went unanswered. Turpin glimpsed Elizabeth kneeling by her bed - and overheard her pray for God to forgive her husband. She begged God for the strength to forgive him for his crime – his mortal sin – too. Turpin did not quite know whether to consider that his wife was full of folly or full of grace.

The outlaw did not quite know either whether he was doing the honourable - or follyful - thing in riding through the night to potentially meet his fate. Marie had all but forsaken him. Why should he not abandon his former lover to her fate? But Turpin had enough blood on his hands already. It was time that he saved, rather than ruined, a life.

Whitechapel.
The smell of soot, sprats and dung hung in the air like the fog. Grey had dropped off his passengers. As much as his arms ached from the long ride, the hackney carriage driver still happily held out his hands to receive the last of his money. As flush as he felt with coin, Grey was too exhausted to treat himself to a hearty meal and drink. Bed called to him, like a harlot with a low-cut dress and beckoning finger.

The lights were dim but still aflame in the tavern, *The Black Prince*. A few carriages, with a stable boy feeding and watering the horses, were lined up outside. Turpin, wary of being recognised at the drinking hole he used to frequent, asked Gill to enter on his own and seek out someone willing to accept a fare. A gangly, swarthy sot lay outside the establishment, dead to the world. His chapped lips were twisted into a smile - or they were contorted, as if he had just suffered a fit. As the highwayman noticed a large fly feasting on a crumb of food lodged in his wispy beard, Turpin found himself strangely envying the wretched figure.

If need be, Turpin was willing to steal a coach or a couple of horses. But thankfully, Gill did not take long to re-appear. He was followed outside by a bleary-eyed coachman, bleary-eyed from either the long night or the long night's drinking. Gill introduced him as Tobias Vardy. The former sailor had grey whiskers, yellow teeth and a rum-stained mouth. Turpin barely understood a word he muttered, due to him slurring his speech or talking in a thick, Norfolk accent.

"I dare say that I underestimated your powers of persuasion, Nat. What did you say in there to recruit someone so quickly?" Turpin posed to his friend.

"I let the money do the talking. Tonight is proving quite expensive."

Let us just hope that we do not pay with our lives too.

Progress was slow. Stars pin-pricked the sky but the night was still as dark as the inside of a hangman's hood. The driver did not wish to risk injury to his horses or damage to his coach. Slow progress was better than no progress at all. Ironically, Turpin was worried about encountering highwaymen on their journey. They would deliver swift justice and retribution to any reprobates who tried to delay them.

Turpin lit a small lamp and asked his companion to hold it aloft, while he satisfied his curiosity and read more of the Frenchman's journal. Even the murderous, womanising rogue blanched at some its contents.

"There is one thing sweeter than bedding a corrupted girl – and that is bedding an uncorrupted girl. Henri Regnard invited me to his estate

to hunt and try out some new firearms he had purchased. But the real sport was pursuing his pretty - but prim - daughter. Minette. Regnard thought he was embracing a friend when we encountered one another. But he was clutching a serpent to his bosom. She wore flowers in her hair and a modest dress, whilst carrying a prayer book, when I first spied the nymph. She was in bloom, or just about to be in bloom. Her cheeks resembled two rosy, ripened apples when I made her blush. The father was almost as innocent and naïve as the daughter when he suggested that Minette should exercise the new pony he had bought her and show their guest the southern grounds of the estate. I was courteous but somewhat aloof initially, treating the young woman like a child. I asked her cursory questions about her interests and education. She duly attempted to prove to me that she was leaving childish notions and activities behind. I slowly but surely thawed. When we came to a stream, we watered our horses. I took off my shirt and bathed myself, cooling myself in the heat of the afternoon sun. She blushed again and was coy, but not that coy. Having noticed her stare at a couple of scars on my torso I began to recount some (fictional) war and duelling stories. I spoke of defending a woman's honour and losing a friend – "he was like a brother to me" – during a skirmish with a group of brigands. The dam burst – and I poured out my finer feelings. I recited some poetry. I dare say her prayer book will now seem dull and didactic, in comparison. I devoutly declared that beauty and grace are one in the same thing. The world can be a cruel place, I argued, but love can and did exist. I hinted at the extent of my wealth. We spoke about art, and I expressed that nothing would give me greater pleasure than seeing some of her sketches (I later saw some her ghastly daubs - but confessed that they had touched my soul). Minette beamed with happiness and pride when I sheepishly revealed that I had never shared my feelings and stories in such a manner before.

I was pleased to see Minette in a more immodest dress later that night, for dinner. For me. We exchanged some clandestine - but telling - looks throughout the evening. Several other women attempted to distract me, or attract me, but I subtly made it clear that I only had eyes for my tender prey. She still endured various pangs of jealousy, which were as precious to me as the gemstones she wore around her nubile neck. We spoke to each other briefly as we gathered for drinks after dinner. But we were in polite society – and acted politely. When I ventured out onto a terrace, I knew that she would follow me, like a puppy dog. The terrace looked out into a far too artificial, or English, garden – but the setting was suitably romantic for the conceited girl. We both leaned against the marble balustrade, beneath a throbbing moon and gleaming vista of stars. Jasmine and roses scented the air.

"*I must confess that I thought you young, a child, when I first met you Minette. But I am not too proud to admit that I was wrong. If you are young, you are also wonderfully wise. Wiser than women who are twice your age... Forgive me, my heart is galloping when I know it should trot. I used to believe that indifference was next to godliness. But I cannot be indifferent when in your company. I cannot ignore my feelings and sweep them away, as a servant would dust... Pray, do not deceive me. The truth is always preferable to deception, no matter how harsh it may be. Tell me, does your heart chime with mine, Minette? Do you feel something similar?*"

As balmy as the evening was, I still noted the pimples on her forearms as I played the pained but passionate soldier. She was breathless when she spoke, her heart in her mouth. I cannot recall her exact response, but her speech resembled dialogue from the kind of tedious and tawdry novels that the English seem to enjoy so much. Indeed, it took a heroic effort on my part not to laugh at myself – and more so her. I do recall the girl uttering the following, though:

"*I want to let you into my heart and into my room,*" *she remarked, her almond eyes becoming a little lascivious, for the first time in her life.*

Just as her words kissed the air - and I squeezed her trembling hand - her father entered like an unwitting - and unwanted - chaperone and joined us on the terrace. But Minette had said enough. The girl desired to be a woman.

Later that evening I entered her room and deflowered the bloom. Despite my lack of sleep and the previous night's exertions I still managed to bag more birds than my host during our shooting expedition the following morning.

I decided to leave that day, much to the sorrow of "my dearest Minette", but I explained that I had received a message containing news that my mother had fallen gravely ill. I was bombarded with letters, as if I were under siege from an army of cannons, shortly after returning home. The first missive contained perfume. The fourth one was stained with tears. I find the latter more attractive and authentic. Her feelings – and grammar – became increasingly muddled. I did not deign to reply to any of the correspondence, of course.

Readers of this journal will verily condemn me for my atrocious and unchivalrous behaviour. But let me present a case for the defence, not that I feel that I should have to justify myself to you. Gods should not have to justify their ways to Man. But did I not teach the girl a valuable lesson? Will her heart not be guarded and hardened against any future gentlemen who wish to take advantage of her? Gentlemen who will promise her the world but give nothing of themselves. Gentlemen who will pay lip-service to chivalry. What was innocent is now experienced. I should be congratulated, rather than castigated. For what if the girl even enjoyed the experience, more than you can imagine or sympathise with? What if she has tasted forbidden fruit and craves more of the same? She could be now closer to being confident and comfortable with vice and immorality. Emancipated and enlightened. Minette may well now devote herself to a life of pleasure. And, to quote Epicurus, "Pleasure is the beginning and end of living happily." Instead of being heart-broken, she will become a breaker of hearts herself...

Claude Gontaut is a wealthy man, perhaps the wealthiest individual in Normandy. He is a farmer and a fine breeder of horses. He also owns vineyards, mines – and mass produces earthenware, cutlery and leather goods. Gontaut is a patron of the arts, funds two schools and recently built a hospital for army veterans. He has been married to the same woman for over two decades and his three children are healthy and happy. He is a generous and gregarious party host - and possesses above-average taste in art and literature. Gontaut is also a pederast.

He thrashes, with a horsewhip, at least one of his staff once a week. He is a bully and a cheat when it comes to business dealings. He once poisoned a freshwater stream in order to compel a neighbouring farmer to sell him his land. The lauded magnate has also just paid me a significant sum of money to murder a man. A priest. The blessed (or not so blessed) Father Jean Rousseau. By all accounts, Rousseau is dull and pious in equal measure. He has – admirably or foolishly – maintained his vows of chastity and poverty. I have heard him been called "a living saint". He is close to God, someone remarked. He will be even closer to the Almighty, by the close of the week, should I succeed. And I will succeed. Rousseau has a wide, squashed face and heavily pock-marked skin. He resembles a toad. Not even my soul is as ugly as his visage, I warrant.

Over the past year Rousseau has been gathering evidence and testimonies, in order to bring a prosecution against Gontaut. He has even interviewed several children who Gontaut abused (most of his victims attended the schools he founded). One wonders if the priest would be so zealous if he was asked to hunt down pederasts in the church. Should his superiors decide to openly accuse and punish Gontaut for his crimes, it will be because they see it as an opportunity to appropriate his land and capital. Or it may be the case that they use the evidence Rousseau has amounted as leverage to extract a donation from Gontaut – to pay for his sins.

But the goodly Father Rousseau will not reach Paris, to meet with the relevant ecclesiastical and state authorities. I have been given the date and route in relation to him journeying to the capital. He will be travelling in a carriage. My intention is to intercept the priest on the road, in an area known to be rife with brigands. Gontaut has instructed me to secure the papers in his possession (the aforementioned evidence). I have duly charged Gontaut an additional fee, that I should have lower myself and behave like a common thief...

The deed, or misdeed, is done. The priest's soul is no longer housed in his unsightly body. If Rousseau was as virtuous as reported – and the afterlife is not a fantasy, comparable to Mount Olympus – then I have sent a man to Heaven. Let us hope that I may be one day rewarded, in a spiritual rather than just financial manner, for such a charitable act. It was telling that Rousseau begged me – rather than God – to spare his wretched life, in the end. I prefer to draw my rapier when going about my business. I am a surgeon, not butcher. Yet, to play out my role as a violent brigand, I hacked my victim to death - splitting his skull open with a meat cleaver. I wore a chef's apron whilst doing so, to prevent my pearl-coloured silk shirt from being stained.

"*I did not commit half the dishonourable acts that Rousseau accused me of,*" Gontaut explained, when I passed on the news and collected the remainder of my fee.

"*That is not my concern. You were sufficiently honourable to pay me and fulfil our contract. That is all that matters,*" I assured him.

I also passed on the priest's papers, containing evidence of Gontaut's indiscretions – albeit I retained some choice testimonies. I became a common thief. Perhaps I will one day debase myself and stoop to blackmail too, if I find that it provides me with the requisite sport…"

An apricot-coloured fringe of light lined the treetops on the horizon. Birdsong began to thread its way through the howling wind. His eyes ached, like fresh bruises. There were words which Turpin was unable to translate, but he could hazard a guess. The highwayman had killed Thomas Morris out of self-preservation. He would kill Pierre Vergier, however, out of a need to protect others. The most uncomfortable aspect of reading the compromising diary was that Turpin recognised shades of own character in the Frenchman. But thankfully not too much, he judged - not quite knowing if he was deceiving himself or not.

15.

Buckhurst Hill.

As Turpin rode through his village, he realised how much more of an effort he could have made to be neighbourly. He was familiar with a few regulars at his tavern and a couple of customers at the butcher's shop, but otherwise the parish must have deemed John Palmer aloof - that the frequent visitor to London looked down upon his country cousins. In contrast, Elizabeth was much liked. She was probably much pitied too, for being married to John Palmer.

Gun metal grey clouds congregated overhead, coming together like a pitchfork wielding mob. A storm seemed to be on the horizon.

Turpin, feeling stiff and as weary as hell, cordially thanked the coachman for his trouble and even paid him extra for the fare. The highwayman hoped that the kind and generous act might earn him some good fortune for the hours ahead. The pouches under Tobias Vardy's eyes appeared large enough to carry the coin he had just been given. The former sailor did not quite know whether he needed a drink or his bed more. His mind was made up when John Palmer offered the coachman a measure of ale on the house, at the local tavern which he owned.

The outlaws entered the stables. Black Bess was a sight for sore eyes. Turpin raised a smile and clasped two hands around the mare's head, as if he were about to plant a wet kiss on her. He patted and stroked the horse's glossy neck. Bess reacted by scraping her hoof and whinnying with delight. She was keen to stretch her legs too. Turpin never had any trouble showing love and affection to his horses. It was people that the outlaw had trouble with. So few souls deserved love and affection. But Elizabeth did, it dawned upon him.

Turpin left Gill to saddle the horses. As he walked from the stables to the house his mood was as grim as the leaden skies. He experienced a presentiment, almost like a visitation, that he would somehow fail in his mercy mission – that either he, or Marie, were destined to perish.

He felt sick, like he had eaten a rotten egg or downed a cup of sour wine. Fear addled his brain. The Frenchman would get the better of him. He had bested the Englishman with a sword. There was no reason to think that he would not do so again.

A pale tendril of smoke unfurled like a ribbon of silk from the chimney. More than once, Turpin had thought about what he could and should say to his wife when they met, rehearsing lines like an actor on his debut. He could die. She deserved some portion of the truth, for once. There would not be time to tell her everything. It was best if she did not know that he was about to risk everything, to save his mistress. Turpin wanted to say sorry to Elizabeth, for a multitude of sins. He wanted to say thank you, for caring for him. It was more than he deserved.

He caught the scent of fresh flowers and thyme, from his wife's flourishing herb garden, as he crossed the threshold. For moment, when he entered the kitchen, Turpin thought that he was staring at someone other than Elizabeth. His wife appeared more pretty than plain. She was wearing her hair down - and was dressed in her best Sunday clothes. A belt accentuated her figure – a figure worth showing off to the world. Her complexion was glowing, sun-kissed from an afternoon spent gardening. Her bible lay on the table, beside her. He realised that if he had to just keep one book in the house it would be that one (or *Gulliver's Travels* or *Hamlet*). Turpin surmised that she had just come back from church. He recalled a line from Vergier's diary, and considered that the arch-deceiver may have been unwittingly telling the truth about something:

"Beauty and grace are one in the same thing."

"You're back," Elizabeth remarked, as a part statement and part question. Her mouth smiled, but her eyes didn't. She did not feel any compulsion to embrace or kiss him, fearing that she would smell drink - or a woman's perfume - on his clothes if she did so.

"Yes. I am afraid I need to go out again. How are you?"

"I am fine," she remarked, in a voice which was somewhat more doleful than someone who was feeling fine. "Do you have business with Nathaniel?"

"Yes, in a way. You look nice today." His voice was a little stilted, like an axel needing oiling, unused as he was perhaps to sincerity.

"I have just returned from church," she replied, confused or suspicious in relation to the compliment. She had received so few compliments from her husband over the years that it was difficult for Elizabeth to recognise or accept them.

Turpin wondered if his wife had prayed for him during church. He needed all the prayers he could receive right now, he judged. And God was more likely to listen to Elizabeth than her husband, quite justifiably. Prayers were not nothing, despite what the evangelical atheists preached. At the very least they were next to nothing. And that was something.

Black Bess whinnied again, outside, calling for him. Turpin was tempted to make sure that Elizabeth knew where he kept his will and coin.

"Do you need to change?"

"Yes," he replied, not realising that she was referring to his besmirched apparel. "Sorry, I need to go," he added. The highwayman was going to promise that he would return soon, but Turpin did not want to make a promise that he couldn't keep. He had lied to her enough. He turned to leave but then turned again, as if suddenly remembering something, and approached his wife. For a moment, Elizabeth was close to flinching or recoiling as her husband strode towards her. But she thankfully found herself returning his embrace. She was also pleasantly surprised to find that his clothes did not smell of drink or perfume.

The embrace lingered. At one point Elizabeth fancied that she was almost holding her husband up. Tears moistened his eyes, like a penitent, but she was unable to view the expression on his face. She thought he mumbled "Sorry" and "I love you" but couldn't be sure. It was unlikely. Part of Turpin did not want to let go. He wanted to hold her even tighter and plant a kiss on her cheek, as a prelude to kissing other parts of her body. But the outlaw needed to go. To be dutiful. To be honourable. To be the Dick Turpin his wife deserved.

Turpin touched the bust of Julius Caesar as he left the house, for good luck, before remembering that Caesar had been assassinated.

Elizabeth gazed through the window and watched as Nathaniel handed Turpin the sword which he kept in a secret compartment in the stables, which she pretended she did not know about.

16.

Their pace remained even, albeit the same could not be said for the surface of the road. Marie held up her new bracelet - decorated with garnet and amethyst and rubies - to what little light there was inside the carriage. William had given the piece of jewellery to his intended the night before. The actress insisted that he should not keep buying her presents – but her face lit-up on receiving the bracelet – and Hervey knew that her sexual appetite and prowess always increased after he spoiled her.

Marie also veritably purred and snuggled up to William when he remarked that the cook at the estate, situated just outside of Norwich, "will provide you with whatever your stomach desires. And I will furnish you with whatever your heart desires, my darling." The actress began to feel like a princess.

She had never travelled to Norfolk before. She had heard that incest was rife among the families living there – and it was not uncommon to encounter certain deformities, such as low foreheads and six digits on a hand. Marie took such reports with a pinch of salt, however. After all, she had encountered plenty of Welshmen and aristocrats over the years and she hadn't observed any notable deformities.

Having courted and been courted by members of the nobility before, the actress was confident that she could win Edward Hervey over. "His bark is now worse that his bite… He has mellowed since retiring from the army," William explained. He warned Marie that his mother may not be so initially hospitable, adding that she had a habit of acting aloof and cold towards all new guests.

"My mother is capable of the odd insensitive comment. It's just her way. Do not take it personally, if it happens," William posited, full knowing that it would happen. They just needed to get this visit over with – and then they could live happily ever after. Surely his father would not cut him off, when he announced his intentions?

"Your mother cannot be as cruel as several theatre critics I could name," Marie replied. "I will be fine."

"I should also warn you that my parents may arrange to place us in separate bedrooms. But like Romeo to your Juliet, I will be willing to scale the walls to your balcony to steal a kiss."

"I understand, my darling. We should respect your parent's rules and wishes. You should not compare us with such tragic lovers, though," the superstitious actress said, as she allowed William to pour her another glass of champagne.

The assassin selected a suitably narrow section of the road, just after a slight bend, at which to position the coach. Any vehicle travelling by would have to stop or slow to a crawl to negotiate their way through.

Despite the overcast skies, the sharp-faced, slim-built Gaspard assured his master that it was unlikely to rain in the next hour or so. There would be little danger of his powder getting damp and his pistols misfiring. Vergier had cause to believe his valet. He had been right about such things on previous occasions.

The horses were happy being idle, both the two dapple mounts heading up the carriage and the large black mare the valet had arranged for Vergier to ride away on, impersonating the highwayman. The punctilious manservant first loaded his master's pistols before loading his own carbine. He fastidiously adjusted the handkerchief around his neck, so he could pull it into place with ease when needed. The Englishman's coach could arrive at any moment. Or they might need to wait for several hours. The readiness was all.

Although his master could often prove impatient, when it came to satisfying his appetites and fending off boredom in town, the former officer was unerringly focussed when it came to his work. Vergier was meticulous in his preparation, clinical in his execution. The valet had grown to admire – and be fearful of his master – immensely. He had served Vergier as an officer, spy and assassin. As Vergier could be as dedicated as a priest to his vocation, Gaspard was as loyal as a disciple. The engraver's son had only ever hesitated to carry out one of his master's orders (during his first month of service, when Vergier instructed his manservant to lock a number of foreign prisoners in a barn, before incinerating the structure). Partly due to the dressing down Gaspard received, the valet had been unstinting in his duties since. The Frenchman told himself that he was being a good patriot whilst carrying out some of the chores for his master. Gaspard had killed for the nobleman. If he was ordered to run a blade through the Englishwoman, even if he discovered she was with child, the valet would obey the instruction, as if he had been asked to pass the salt.

The faithful Breton had even promised to serve his master after he passed, by overseeing the publication of his diaries. He would be Tiro, to Vergier's Cicero.

"I may have a few mewling bastards running around out there, Gaspard, that I am blissfully unaware of - but my diaries will provide my true legacy. Rather than my seed, these pages house my soul. My name will live on, after I am gone, through my words and deeds. My diary will at first shock the world – but there will also be those precious few readers who will be enlightened and emancipated by my confessions… I will also leave you the means to publish the book yourself, should any publisher lack the spine to publish and be damned."

A breeze caused the dust to swirl, branches to sway, leaves to tremble and a lock of his hair two twitch. Pierre Vergier appeared calm yet determined – imperious and impervious – as he stared into the space that the Englishman's carriage would at some point occupy. The coachmen would be mere chaff. He would shoot them without hesitation or bothering to register their reactions. They were little more than livestock – destined to be slaughtered. Vergier would be keen to observe - and absorb - the expression on Hervey's face when he confronted death. He would watch his pupils dilate, his complexion grow ashen. The assassin had sent scores of people to the grave. Some appealed to a sense of mercy and compassion, others offered Vergier money to appeal to his greed. The latter was more likely to succeed, but never did. Vergier prided himself on being a man of honour and fulfilling his contracts. A swathe of his victims would cross themselves and pray to God, as they looked into the eyes of the Devil, but at no point did the Almighty ever intercede, Vergier noted. The assassin thought the smell of gunpowder as morish as caviar, after a shooting. He enjoyed the ceremony of cleaning the blood from his blade and polishing his sword afterwards, so no trace of the crime remained. A well-crafted rapier was the perfect marriage of elegance and function. A sword needed to be bloodied every now and then, to satisfy its thirst.

Vernier stared down at his garb and pursed his lips. The Frenchman wryly thought to himself that the famed highwayman could be reckoned courageous, just for daring to wear an outfit so out of tune with the latest style in Paris.

Turpin needed to be mindful of both the speed and stamina of their mounts. Take care of your horse and they will rightly take care of you in return. The wind blew in more directions than a politician's loyalties and occasionally Turpin reached up to press his hat down upon his head. Low, menacing clouds continued to scour the sky. But still a storm or shower had yet to come to pass. Perhaps it would not rain, the highwayman mused. Perhaps Hervey would take another route, and all would be well. Turpin had a plan to present the diary to Edward Hervey. The old soldier may not openly admit to the atrocity he committed, but he would muster the resources to apprehend the assassin – or serve as judge and executioner. Turpin wondered whether he should join the prospective hunt for Vergier. The fox could not be allowed to escape.

The two men rode on, joining the main artery between the counties of Essex and Norfolk, an amalgamation of hope and trepidation.

The Frenchman heard the coach and even sensed tremors in the ground before espying the vehicle. Vergier permitted himself a smile, recognising the coat of arms on the side of the carriage. Behind him, Gaspard wiped his perspiring palms on his breeches, in preparation for grabbing his carbine.

A blunderbuss sat in between the two coachmen, Peter Fenton and James Skinner. The former had worked in service to the Hervey family for as long as he could remember. His mother had been a kitchen and his father a gardener to Edward Hervey. Having swapped stories with other coachmen, Fenton realised that he could have worked in worse households. The flame-haired, freckled James Skinner was new to his duties. He was the son of a quartermaster, who had served in Edward Hervey's regiment. The former General, who still maintained that he had a duty of care to his soldiers, instructed his son to take the young man on. The coachmen worked well together. They bunked together and drank together. Unfortunately, they would soon die together.

Fenton pulled on the reins and slowed the carriage. Inside, Hervey's features tightened in irritation. He had given explicit instructions not to stop for any beggars or food vendors on the road.

Gaspard offered a friendly wave to the Englishman. Vergier's countenance was welcoming, cordial, even as he plunged his hands into his deep coat pockets and retrieved his pistols. Before either of the coachmen had time to reach for the blunderbuss they were gunned down. Two shots. Two fatal chest wounds. Vergier's taut face, behind a haze of smoke, betrayed little or no emotion as he went about his business. Pansy-shaped blotches of blood stained their linen shirts. Skinner slumped forward and then fell from his perch. Gaspard moved quickly to grab the bridle of one of the carriage's horses, to prevent the creature from bolting and potentially stealing their prize away. A smattering of birds - sparrows, thrushes, larches – took flight and darted out of the nearby trees upon hearing the sudden, abrasive shots. The assassin took no notice of the wildlife, however, as he raised the black mask and unsheathed his sword.

Marie let out a piercing, almost operatic scream upon hearing the gun shots. Hervey just about fell short of doing the same. The cavalry officer had looked good in his dress uniform, but even his father could not boast that his son was an accomplished or valiant soldier. The army did not mourn his decision to resign from his commission. Edward Hervey paid for his son to enter the army, at an elevated rank, and paid for him to leave. Marie could not quite tell if William was reaching for the door of the cab to abscond, or lock it, when the point of the rapier came through the open window, falling just short of her lover's lily-white throat.

"Out," Vergier evenly commanded, rather than barked. He thought to keep his words to a minimum, lest he betray his accent to the audience of the actress. "Stay," he added, pointing at Marie.

"Please, take whatever you want," Hervey remarked, after suffering a catch in his throat. He had alighted from the cab and stood before the supposed highwayman, his legs and bladder nearly giving way. Out of the corner of his eye the aristocrat observed the slain coachman, laid out on the road like a stain. If it was at all possible, Hervey's complexion went a shade paler.

Vergier remained silent, disgusted that the alleged nobleman should behave with such cowardice and servility. He deserved to die, autonomous of Montbard's wishes.

On the other side of the coach Gaspard glowered through the window, despising Marie for both being English and a woman, and said the word "valuables" whilst holding out his hand. The traumatised actress complied with the instruction, believing that it would prove useless to beg, or flutter her extended eyelashes at the brusque outlaw.

The temperature dropped, but that wasn't what necessarily caused a chill to run down William Hervey's spine. The purple-black sky darkened even more. A brace of leaves fell overhead from an elm tree. Perhaps it was the first day of Autumn. Hervey noticed the shape of the highwayman's mask change, as if the villain were grinning beneath it. The assassin drew his sword back, ready to thrust. He would aim the point of the blade at the Englishman's chest, with the intention of scything through his heart and/or lungs. Marie lifted an un-bejewelled hand to her mouth (Gaspard had plucked the rings from her fingers), in preparation to suppress a sob or scream. Vergier's almost equitable countenance suddenly became animated above the line of his mask. His eyebrows formed a pronounced V-shape and his aspect exploded with such fire, that one could have imagined Hephaestus having set-up a furnace behind his pupils. Hervey cowered, squirmed and raised his hands – but remained rooted to the spot. Damned.

The tamp of hooves could be felt upon the road again. Dust spat up from the ground, near to the assassin, as Turpin fired his pistol, in hope of distracting the Frenchman and preventing him from stabbing his rival.

The outlaw kicked his heels into the flanks of his powerful mount once more. Should Turpin have asked the mare to gallop into the belly of a whale, Black Bess would have done so. The creature's breathing was laboured, having been ridden throughout the day, and her usually pristine coat displayed a patina of sweat, but the horse still held its head high in determination, like its owner.

Nathaniel Gill veered towards the side of the road to ride towards the gun-wielding figure standing next to the window of the coach. Both men discharged their carbines, but both missed. Initially Gaspard's visage was a mixture of astoundment and resentment – at witnessing the two riders appear out of nowhere to attack them – but then fear flooded his heart and face.

"What do we do if Vergier has any confederates with him?" Gill asked his friend, when they had set off earlier.

"Kill the bastards. All of them," Turpin replied, without hesitation.

Gaspard, realising that there would be no time to reload, decided to retreat, with the intention of retrieving a loaded pistol, which he had placed on the seat of his carriage.

Gill was even slicker with sweat than his fatigued mount, Hector. Thankfully the skilled horseman had ridden him before, however, and knew what he was capable of. His quarry ran. He was close to the safety of the carriage, but not close enough. Gill slowed Hector and wheeled the horse around, so its rump slammed into the retreating Frenchman. Gaspard was thrown forward, crashing into the side of the carriage. The valet's aquiline nose broke, and he fell to the ground, groaning. Gill dismounted, snorting. The brawny highwayman was tempted to dispatch the Frenchman by bashing his skull in, using the stock of carbine to do so. But then he worried that he might damage the valuable weapon. Instead, Gill drew his dagger, which he usually used for cutting up his sausages, grabbed the valet by his hair and ran the blade across the Frenchman's neck as if he were a slaughtering a pig and draining the blood to make a batch of blood pudding.

Meanwhile, Turpin had inserted himself and Black Bess between his opponent and Hervey. The nobleman remained as slack jawed as a peasant - bewildered and frightened. He had more questions than answers. Indeed, he didn't have any answers.

"What the hell is happening?" Hervey ejaculated.

"Just stay behind me William and keep out of the way," Turpin replied, without taking his eyes off the assassin.

"Do as he says, William," the actress ordered, impatiently, her voice even more commanding than the highwayman's. Hervey nodded and obeyed. The exchange was a glimpse into their future married life.

Turpin dismounted.

Vergier was surprised, to say the least, at the circumstances of encountering the Englishman again. Yet his expression remained impassive, if slightly curdled. He did not wish to concede that he was no longer in control of the scene, or that he had been outflanked by the commoner.

It wasn't quite like looking in the mirror. No, not quite. The two men, clad in similar yet different apparel, stood opposite one another. Turpin thought that the Frenchman was more of both a dandy highwayman and butcher highwayman, familiar as he was with the assassin's past.

Given the recent activity, it remained strangely, deathly quiet for a few moments, before Turpin drew his sword and Vergier broke the silence.

"I did not consider that you would go to such lengths to arrange a rematch, Englishman," the aristocrat remarked, not without a little sangfroid, after pulling down his mask.

Hervey could be heard to gasp in the background and was about to splutter out some words, but Marie duly silenced him.

"I am a bad loser," Turpin drily replied, shrugging slightly.

"That is a shame, seeing that it unlikely that the result now will prove anything different to the previous outcome."

Gill caught his friend's eye and pointedly marked his loaded carbine. But his companion shook his head. Turpin needed to face the devil again, to somehow be brave and honourable. The itch needed scratching.

"This will not be an exhibition bout. I will not have to be so polite."

"Neither will I," Vergier spat out, either sneering or smiling. "May I just ask one thing first, to satisfy my curiosity? Tell me, how did you come to be here?"

"You should not be so careless - and leave your diary lying about."

It was the Englishman's turn to smile, much to the Frenchman's chagrin. Vergier seethed, his usually serpentine eyes widening in disbelief and alarm. It was as if someone had stolen his bible. Deconsecrated it. He bared his teeth, in a grimace or rictus. Thoughts scrambled around in his brain, like drowning sailors trying to cling on to an upturned lifeboat. His rapier wanted to taste blood, more than ever.

Perhaps sensing the ire and desperation of the Frenchman, Gill raised his carbine and tempered any impulse the assassin might have had to attack the highwayman. Turpin removed his coat and neatly folded it, before placing it on a patch of grass by the side of the road.

The lowborn outlaw raised his sword once more, in the manner of a gentleman.

"I cannot fault your courage, for wishing to face me again. I bested you once and I will best you again. But courage can often be deemed foolhardiness," Vergier pronounced, as he swished his weapon around in his hand, to loosen up his wrist. All was not lost, he reasoned. His strategy would be to manoeuvre his combatant around, so he was in striking distance of the figure carrying the carbine. He would aim to wound and kill both dogs in quick succession. There was no possibility of the Englishman outfencing him. He could even still succeed in his mission to end Hervey. He would of course need to silence the whore too.

The two men now stood only a few feet apart, the tips of their weapons nearly touching.

Rain began to pepper the air, auguring a heavy shower. Vergier thought to himself that, if he could draw out the sport, the burly Englishman's carbine could misfire from the rain - and his advantage would increase.

Turpin suddenly paused, reaching for his hat, as though he had forgotten to remove it. Instead of putting the cocked hat with his coat, however, he threw it in the direction of his opponent. The outlaw had employed a similar tactic during a tavern brawl, a few years back, in order to disorientate a knife-carrying drunk who had squared up to him. For a moment or two Vergier was similarly disorientated. Turpin pounced. With a sudden backslash of his sword, he swatted the Frenchman's fine blade out of the way and moved inside. Turpin grabbed his opponent's wrist, to the hand carrying his sword. The skilful assassin recovered, though, and reached for Turpin's sword arm. The two combatants grappled for a few seconds, although it felt longer for all those concerned, before the highwayman butted the Frenchman, splitting open the bridge of his nose. Still Vergier clung on. But Turpin released his grip on the assassin's hand. Vergier would now bring his weapon to bear. He would slam the guard across Englishman's face and then turn the rapier on his confederate – catching him unaware, unable to aim and fire the carbine in time. Vergier would react quickly. But he was not quick enough. Before the Frenchman could deliver his blow, Turpin had reached his free hand behind his back to retrieve the letter knife tucked into his breeches. He thrust the makeshift weapon upwards, its stiletto-like point skewering his opponent's chin, mouth and brain. Blood dribbled down the gleaming blade, like tears. The assassin perished with an acute sense of shock still shaping his expression. It was difficult to tell whether the shock derived from being bested by the commoner, or that he had used his letter knife to carry out the deed.

Turpin knew that he could not outfence the aristocrat, but the Englishman could outfight him.

"Don't feel too disconsolate. You fought well," the highwayman remarked to the corpse, with not a little sardony.

17.

Epilogue.

The heavy rain held off or fell elsewhere. Gill gave Hervey the remainder of the brandy in his flask, an uncommonly generous act for the highwayman, to help settle the nobleman's nerves. More than anyone else, Hervey considered that he had endured an ordeal. And it was all the more distressing for not knowing why. Questions needed to be answered. Turpin showed him the relevant diary entries. The ex-officer may not have been able to ride or shoot terribly well, but he was fluent in French. A torrent of gratitude succeeded a torrent of shock and disbelief. When Hervey asked John Palmer how he had come by the diary, Marie insisted that her friend was tired - and it was best not to ask too many questions. Again, he thought it wise to obey his would-be wife.

Turpin arranged for Gill to drive their carriage onwards to Hervey's family estate. They would also take the bodies of Fenton and Skinner with them. They deserved a Christian burial. Vergier and his accomplice deserved less of a Christian burial. Gill would temporarily hide the cadavers in the woods – and then incinerate them on his way back. "Burn the bastards. Ashes to ashes, as the good book says." Hervey would explain events to his father and the old soldier could deal with the Vicomte de Montbard as he saw fit. Turpin would take the remaining carriage and horses to a coaching inn just south of their location. He would then continue to take his own mounts home. He declined an invitation to join Hervey at his estate.

"I owe you my life, John. You should be rightly lauded. I should reward you," the aristocrat remarked, with a new-found respect for the landlord and butcher.

"A good deed is its own reward. I have no desire to see my name in the newspapers," John Palmer argued, in reply. Turpin decided that he could not now verily rob Hervey. His trip to London had indeed been expensive. But worth it.

Before setting off, Marie was mindful of sharing a few words with her old acquaintance in private. She had questions which needed to be answered too, although she sensed that the highwayman was not in the mood to address all of them. She had perhaps never been as attracted to Turpin, or any man, as she was then. The courtesan even envied the man's wife. Desire and devotion stirred in her being, like a pot simmering on the stove. The actress felt indebted to her friend – and if the virile outlaw suggested to pay him in kind and remain his mistress, she would have.

"I am not sure how I should thank you," Marie whispered, as her scintillating, wide eyes stared up at Turpin - and she prettily tucked a few strands of blonde hair behind her bejewelled ears. Desirous and desirable.

"Just do not send me an invitation to your wedding, or introduce me to any more actors," he drily responded. "But I wish you well Marie Harley, or I should say that I will always think of you as Mary Hardy."

"And I wish you well too, John Palmer. Or I should say that I will always think of you as Dick Turpin. We had some fun. I am not sure whether I seduced you, or you seduced me, but the outcome was the same," the actress posed, regaining her luscious, playful smile.

"William seems a good man. If he isn't, then I have every confidence that you will turn him into one."

"And what about you, Richard? Are you a good man?"

"I'm trying. I'm failing, of course, but at least I am now trying."

Turpin nodded and courteously lifted his hat to a few of his neighbours as he trotted through the village on Black Bess, with Hector in tow. He even exchanged pleasantries with Oswald Russell, although he did not allow the dullard to detain him for too long. Things hadn't changed that much. The outlaw felt tired, but not as weary as usual. He would take the next fortnight off. Gill should visit London and continue to court Sally. It seemed as if his friend would marry the girl, for better or for worse. Turpin would rest, read and spend time with Elizabeth. He would take her for a drink in one of the finer establishments in the county. He would ask his man at the butcher shop to provide some prime cuts. He would make love to her.

The highwayman drew out Vergier's letter knife and caught his reflection in the blade. He no longer appeared melancholy, or roguish. Turpin was tempted to keep the talisman for good luck. It would also, of course, serve as a useful letter opener. But the thief settled on selling the valuable item on. Hopefully it would prove a talisman through Colman paying a fair price for it.

Turpin unbuckled his sword and put his guns away. He tended to the horses - settling them in the stables, feeding and watering the goodly creatures – before venturing into the main house. Elizabeth did not notice her husband standing in the doorway of the kitchen. He beheld his beautiful, graceful wife. She was still wearing her hair down. The dress she was wearing he now deemed his favourite dress. There was much he should be thankful for, he felt. Turpin recalled a line from *The Rape of Lock*:

"Charm strikes the sight, but merit wins the soul."

Elizabeth turned around. Her husband looked different. Perhaps it was because he was smiling, contentedly. She imagined that he must have been out drinking all afternoon with Nathaniel.

"Everything fine?" his wife asked.

"No," Turpin replied - and then briefly paused, grinning, whilst the truth dawned upon him. "Things are better than fine."

End Note.

Readers with just a cursory knowledge of Dick Turpin will realise that this is largely a work of fiction. Although we know plenty about the highwayman - particularly the events surrounding his capture, trial and death – Turpin has become more legend than man since the publication of William Harrison Ainsworth's novel *Rookwood*. I have added to the legend, rather than historical record. My Turpin is part Raffles, part Robin Hood, part Richard Sharpe – with a peppering of Flashman. He is also his own man, or legend. Nathaniel Gill, Joseph Colman and Pierre Vergier are complete fictions. Turpin's wife was called Elizabeth, however, and the outlaw was involved in the violent robbery at Earlsbury Farm. The highwayman was also responsible for the death of Thomas Morris. Should you be interested in reading more about the man - and legend - then I can recommend *Dick Turpin: The Myth of the English Highwayman*, by James Sharpe.

England either found or increased its swagger during the 18th century – and at the heart of things was its capital. London was rife with alcoholism and venereal disease, which is not to say that its inhabitants were not partial to other vices. Prosperity and privation, decadence and depravity lived cheek by jowl. Should you be interested in finding out more about life in the capital during the period then I can recommend *London in the 18th Century* by Jerry White, *Dr Johnson's London* by Liza Picard and *English Society in the Eighteenth Century* by Roy Porter.

Having written books set during Ancient Rome and the First Crusade it has been quite a departure to write about Dick Turpin in some ways. But it has been an enjoyable departure. Do please get in touch should you have enjoyed *Turpin's Assassin*, or any of my other books. It's always nice to wake up to an email or review from a reader. You can follow me at @rforemanauthor on Twitter or I can be contacted at richard@sharpebooks.com

Dick Turpin will return in *Turpin's Rival*.

Richard Foreman.

Printed in Poland
by Amazon Fulfillment
Poland Sp. z o.o., Wrocław
17 September 2022

4022f4d5-f6a6-4fdc-8b70-150f39cb41e4R01